Lydia looked around. Everyone was watching her. And Lydia knew that they all thought she was guilty. Even Frankie didn't believe her. Lydia couldn't stand any more. Her eyes stung with unshed, unwelcome tears. All at once her cheeks were wet and Lydia knew she was crying.

'Sir, can I go to the toilet, please?' Lydia whispered.

Mr Fine frowned down at her. 'Go on, then. But hurry up.'

Lydia stood up and walked slowly to the door, her head bent so that no-one could see her face, no-one would catch her eye. Her hand had just reached the door handle when behind her, very softly, very simply, someone called out, 'Thief!'

THIEF!

MALORIE BLACKMAN

CORGI BOOKS

THIEF!
A CORGI BOOK : 0 552 52808 0

First published in Great Britain by Doubleday,
a division of Random House Children's Books

PRINTING HISTORY
Doubleday edition published 1995
Corgi edition published 1995

9 10 8

Corgi Books are published by Random House Children's Books,
61–63 Uxbridge Road, London W5 5SA,
a division of The Random House Group Ltd,
in Australia by Random House Australia (Pty) Ltd,
20 Alfred Street, Milsons Point, Sydney, NSW 2061, Australia,
in New Zealand by Random House New Zealand Ltd,
18 Poland Road, Glenfield, Auckland 10, New Zealand
and in South Africa by Random House (Pty) Ltd,
Endulini, 5a Jubilee Road, Parktown 2193, South Africa.

Set in 11/14pt Linotype Plantin by
Kestrel Data, Exeter.

Printed and bound in Great Britain by
Cox & Wyman Ltd, Reading, Berkshire.

For Neil, with love
And for Mum and Ma, Roma and Eddie
*And **MLO***

One

A Decision To Make

'Anne, I can't do it. It'd be stealing.' Lydia Henson stared at her friend. Then she smiled uncertainly. 'You're joking – right?'

Anne narrowed her eyes. 'I might have guessed. I said to the others you'd be too much of a coward. You London folk are all the same. All talk and no action.'

'That's not fair,' Lydia protested.

The two girls watched each other. The silence in the assembly hall was deafening.

'Look, it's not really stealing,' Anne said with exasperation. 'All you have to do is keep the sports cup in your locker until this time tomorrow. Then just put it back and no-one will ever know you took it in the first place.'

Lydia stared at her own reflection in the glass-fronted cup cabinet. Black plaits tied back in a pony-tail and round, worried, dark-brown eyes shone back at her. Just an average face at the best of times, but right now it looked nervous – almost scared. Lydia looked past her reflection into the cabinet. Small silver-coloured cups for swimming, individual achievement, teamwork and a host of other school activities decorated the wall cabinet's three shelves. And there, holding pride of place in the middle of the cabinet, was the best all-rounder's sports cup.

'If I take it, someone's bound to spot it's missing,' Lydia said unhappily.

'No, they won't. We've each taken it for a day and no-one has ever even noticed,' Anne replied. 'Besides, no-one's going to bother with a sports cup in the middle of the winter term.'

'But it's stealing,' Lydia whispered.

'Not if you only take it for one day. Besides, do you want to be in our group or don't you?' Anne frowned, folding her arms across her chest.

And that was the problem, because they both knew that Lydia wanted to belong. She wanted to belong to the Cosmics very much indeed. And Anne was the leader of the Cosmics, so she had the final say as to who could join and who couldn't.

Lydia looked at the sports cup which glinted in the fluorescent lights of the assembly hall.

'So each of you has already done this?' Lydia said, chewing slowly on her bottom lip.

'I've already said that, haven't I? Frankie has. Maxine has. So has Bharti. I have. *Everyone* has. Now, are you going to do it or not?' Anne flicked her wavy, blond hair out of her eyes with an impatient hand. She began to stroll up and down, casting Lydia a studied, watchful look.

'Anne, I . . . I'm not sure . . .'

The sudden noise of one of the assembly hall doors opening was like the crack of a whip behind them.

Anne scooted to the side of the nearby stage and ducked down – only just in time. Lydia wasn't so lucky. Old Baldie, the caretaker, popped his head round the door, looking first one way then the other.

'Oi! What're you doing in this hall? You know it's out of bounds after school.' Old Baldie entered the hall and stood by the door glaring at Lydia.

He was a tall man, as thin as a noodle and with a face that was so sallow it was just about the same colour. His grey-white hair – what there was of it – waved and wandered all over the sides of his head. Flecks of black here and there in his hair made it look as if black pepper had been sprinkled liberally onto a mound of salt.

'Well? What are you waiting for? Christmas?' snapped Old Baldie.

Lydia glanced at Anne who was squatting down at the side of the stage. Anne placed a finger over her lips and shook her head.

'Sorry, Mr Balding,' Lydia said quickly.

'Shift then!' Old Baldie said with impatience.

Lydia quickly headed for the door furthest away

from the caretaker. If he chose to report her, Lydia knew she'd be in major trouble but she couldn't regret the interruption. Luckily it seemed as if she was going to get away with it. Old Baldie switched off the lights. Lydia made her way along the quad perimeter towards the school gates. She glanced over her shoulder as she walked. Old Baldie was still watching her, his arms folded and a scowl deepening the lines of his face. Then he crossed the quad and walked away in the opposite direction. Lydia slowed down but didn't stop. She heard the assembly hall doors click open behind her.

'Lydia! Lydia, wait!' Anne hissed from behind her.

With a silent sigh, Lydia stopped walking and turned around. Anne ran up to her.

'Old Baldie's a real long streak of misery,' Anne muttered.

Lydia smiled. She'd never heard that expression before. She looked at Anne and her smile faded away to nothing. She looked around. The caretaker had disappeared.

He's probably racing back for his tea, Lydia thought, dejected.

She'd been hoping he'd march her right out of the school, locking the gates behind her. That would've been so wonderful! Lydia sniffed, hugging her coat tighter around her. The freezing November wind was trying to blow straight through her. She glanced up at the mid-grey sky. She hadn't seen one scrap of clear, sunny sky since she and her family had moved to Yorkshire. At least, that's what it felt like.

'It's all right. Old Baldie's gone,' Anne said. 'Come on, now's your chance.'

'Oh, Anne, I . . . Are you sure I won't get caught?' Lydia said.

She didn't walk back to the assembly hall. Her feet didn't want to move.

'Of course you won't. *We* didn't.' Anne's smile was broad. 'Does that mean you're going to do it?'

In the long pause that followed, the howling wind around them began to drop. A sudden thought had Lydia smiling inwardly with intense relief.

'How do I get the cup out of the cabinet? Surely the cabinet will be locked?' Lydia fought to keep the grin off her face.

Maybe she could get out of it after all!

'Ah, we Cosmics know a little secret about the cabinet,' Anne said excitedly.

Lydia's heart sank down to the heels of her socks.

'If you bang upwards on the underside of the cabinet, the left door will fly open. Then you can reach in and get the cup. When you shut the cabinet door afterwards, it'll lock automatically.'

'Anne . . . can't I do something else? I'll do

anything else. If I get caught and my mum and dad find out . . .' Lydia trailed off miserably. She dreaded to think *what* they would do.

Anne's eyes narrowed. 'Lydia, you've got a decision to make. I thought we'd be doing you a favour by letting you join our group, but if you don't want to belong that's up to you. The choice is yours.' And with that, Anne marched away.

'Anne, wait, please . . .'

Lydia was left staring after her helplessly. As Lydia watched, Anne strode out of the school gates and turned up the road. Lydia looked around. She'd never heard the school so quiet. Now that the wind had died down, there was no sound at all – just the rasp of her own anxious breathing.

Lydia walked slowly back into the assembly hall, her feet dragging. Closing the door very quietly behind her, she automatically reached out for the light switch. Her hand was on it before she remembered Old Baldie.

'Lydia, what are you doing?' she muttered to herself.

The hall was in semi-darkness with the lights off. There was just enough daylight coming in from outside through the high windows to cast silver-grey streaks of light throughout the assembly hall. Lydia started to walk across to the trophy cabinet but her shoes clicked and echoed on the wooden parquet floor like tap-shoes.

Raising her heels, Lydia tiptoed the rest of the way, wincing as even the soles of her shoes still made a noise.

And there was the sports cup. It now looked dull and shadowy in the half light of the hall.

'What should I do?' Lydia whispered.

If she took the cup and could put it back without being found out, she'd be part of the Cosmics. Anne had started the Cosmics and it hadn't taken Lydia long to learn that *everyone* wanted to belong to Anne's group. Lydia suspected it had more to do with the fact that Anne's dad owned the local electronics shop than for any other reason. That meant Anne always brought in the latest gadgets from her dad's shop for the Cosmics to use – tape recorders and electronic filofaxes, CD Walkmans and the latest miniature video game sets. She'd even brought in a camcorder once. Anne had them all.

Lydia didn't care about that so much. She wanted to belong to the Cosmics because then she'd be in the same secret club as Frances – or Frankie as she made everyone call her. Anne, Bharti and Maxine were all right – although Anne was a bit too bossy for Lydia's liking – but Frankie was the real reason Lydia wanted to join the Cosmics. Lydia really liked Frankie.

Frankie had volunteered to take care of Lydia from Lydia's first day at Collivale School and now they were best friends. It felt like they'd been best friends for ever instead of just for three weeks. Lydia had found someone like her: someone who loved comics and carrots, someone who hated anything with cabbage in it and who thought that circus clowns were boring.

'So, take the cup,' Lydia told herself.

It was the only way to keep her new friends, to become a part of this strange, new school. If she didn't take it, Anne would delight in telling everyone just how much of a chicken she was. Lydia could hear Anne already.

'. . . all that talk and she couldn't even take the cup. These Londoners . . .'

Lydia sighed deeply. Whichever way she turned, there seemed to be nowhere to go. She stared at the cup cabinet, hating it.

Get it over with, she thought miserably.

But to steal . . .

But to lose her friends . . .

It was getting darker now. Lydia shivered. She gathered all of her rapidly disappearing courage to her like a winter coat. Stepping forward, she pulled at the cabinet doors. They were locked. Taking a deep breath and with the fingers of her left hand crossed, Lydia banged her right fist upwards to meet the underside of the cup cabinet. The left glass door sprung silently open – just as Anne had said it would.

'Oh no!' Lydia said, dismayed. She jumped as the tiny words echoed to fill the assembly hall. Lydia's left fingers slowly uncrossed. The sports cup was now almost completely shrouded in shadow. Lydia stretched out her hand. Tentatively she touched the handle of the cup. She couldn't get a good grip on it. Her fingers slid down it. Her palms were sweating. Lydia took another step forward. She wiped her perspiring forehead, then wiped her wet hand on her school coat. Her heart was about to burst out of her chest.

This was it. The choice was simple.

Take the cup . . . or lose her friends.

Two

Daniel Henson

'Mum? Dad? Can I ask you a question?' Lydia asked. She speared three peas on her plate with her fork, careful not to look up.

'Go on then,' Dad said.

Lydia thought hard, searching for the right words to say without giving away too much.

'If . . . if someone told you that you had to do something you didn't want to do, would you still do it?'

'That would depend on who had asked me, what they'd asked me to do and why they'd asked me to do it,' Dad replied warily. 'Why?'

Lydia risked a glance at her mum and dad.

'No reason. I just wondered.' She shrugged.

Mum gave Lydia a sharp look. 'Have you been offered something at school that you shouldn't have been offered?'

'Of course not,' Lydia said, shocked.

'You haven't had some strange person stopping

their car and offering you a lift, have you?' Mum asked quickly.

Lydia stared at her mum.

'For goodness sake, dear! As Danny would say – take a chill pill!' said Dad. 'Lydia has brains enough to know that she shouldn't accept lifts or anything else from strangers.'

Mum took a deep breath. 'So what's this all about then?' she asked, her voice calmer.

'Honestly!' Dad shook his head.

'It was just a . . . a hypothetical question,' Lydia said.

'Hhmm! Then I would say that if you're not sure whether or not to do something, you should let your conscience decide for you,' said Mum.

Lydia considered. That didn't help her very much. Besides, it was too late to ask for advice now. What was done was done.

'So how was your day, Lydia?'

Lydia chewed on her bottom lip. Her head was bent over her dinner plate so she missed the look which passed between her mum and dad.

'Oh, it was all right – I suppose.'

'You don't sound too sure.' Dad raised an eyebrow.

'It's just that . . .'

'Just that what?' Dad prompted when Lydia said nothing else.

'It . . . it doesn't matter,' Lydia sighed.

'Lydia . . . we know all this has been difficult for you,' Mum said slowly. 'You've had to leave all your friends and your old school behind and I know how happy you were there . . .'

'It's all right, Mum – honest,' Lydia said quickly. 'It's prettier up here than in London and Collivale School is OK.'

Lydia hadn't meant to make her mum feel bad about moving them to Tarwich in Yorkshire. Mum had been promoted by her company but the only snag was that her new job was out of London. Mum and Dad had said it was an opportunity too good to miss. So here they were, three weeks in Tarwich and only just beginning to get to know the people in the small town.

'Have you made lots of friends?' Mum asked eagerly.

'Oh, yes.' Lydia crossed her fingers under the dinner table. 'I've got a new best friend, Frankie, and I go around with her and Maxine and Bharti and Anne, and lots of the others in the class talk to me . . .'

'Oh, that's all right then,' Mum smiled. 'Don't worry, Lydia – you'll soon settle in. Pretty soon you won't ever want to leave. My boss was telling me that Tarwich is the kind of place that gets into your blood. Very few people move away from here.'

Lydia smiled weakly. She couldn't imagine why anyone in their right mind would want to spend their whole life in a place like Tarwich. There was probably something very funny-peculiar in the water which gave all the grown-ups brain fade or something. That would explain a lot!

'Danny, chew your food with your mouth shut, please,' Mum said patiently.

Lydia glanced at her brother with irritation. Danny smiled back at her and opened his mouth wider to display mushed-up peas combined with bits of half-chewed sausage and mashed potatoes. It looked disgusting!

'Daniel Henson, that's quite enough of that,' Mum said sternly.

'Yeuk! It's enough to put you off food for life.' Dad wrinkled up his nose.

Lydia scowled at Danny. He was only ten and already he was a serious pain. What would he be like when he was twice his age? Twice the aggravation? Lydia watched her younger brother wolf down his food. She was getting less and less hungry by the second!

'Danny, you're going to get raging indigestion if you carry on like that. Don't eat so fast,' said Mum.

'But I have to,' Danny protested.

'Why? Your food's not going to run away, you know,' said Dad.

'I have to finish fast before I lose my appetite!' grinned Danny, shovelling another forkful into his mouth.

Mum and Dad looked at each other and burst out laughing.

'Danny, sometimes you talk some real foolishness!' said Mum.

'And that's another reason I don't like it up here.' Danny wrinkled up his nose. 'They all take the mickey out of the way I talk.'

'They'll soon get bored doing that,' said Dad. 'Just be patient.'

'And in the meantime you can always tease them back about the way *they* speak.' Mum winked.

'That hardly solves the problem, dear,' Dad said mildly.

Mum looked ashamed. 'True. Danny, ignore what I just said!'

'I do that anyway.' Danny shook out more tomato ketchup over his food.

'Less of that, you cheeky toad!' Mum tweaked Danny's ear. 'And slow down! You won't lose your appetite before you've finished your food – I promise you!'

Lydia looked at Mum and Dad and her brother Danny. For all Danny's whining, he was coping better with the move to Tarwich than she was. It was all so strange and new. She still couldn't get used to looking out of her bedroom window and seeing the moors stretching out beyond the neighbouring houses, towards the horizon. And in the still of the night, she could hear the river rushing and rumbling past their back garden. Lydia longed for houses and yet more houses as far as the eye could see and the rumble of traffic past their house, not a river. She missed London terribly.

'Danny, I'm not going to tell you again,' Mum said crossly as he continued to chew with his mouth open.

Lydia glared at her brother, annoyed at having her reverie disrupted. Danny really was too gross! She looked down at her dinner plate again, her fork still in her hand.

'Lydia, is something wrong?' Dad leant forward.

'What? Er . . . no, I'm fine.' Lydia tried to smile, but her face felt as if it was twisting horribly instead of smiling, so she gave up the attempt.

'Are you sure?'

Lydia nodded. 'I think I'll go to bed early. I'm just a little bit tired.'

'But you haven't finished your dinner. I squeezed lemon juice over your peas and potatoes, just the way you like it.' Mum frowned.

'No thanks, Mum. I'm not very hungry,' Lydia said.

'I don't know why I bother, I really don't.' Mum sat back in her chair, annoyed. 'I rush home to have dinner with my family only to find that my daughter isn't hungry and my son eats like a cement mixer . . .'

'Off you go, Lydia, while your mum is exercising her jaw.' Dad winked.

'I heard that!' Mum tweaked Dad's ear too.

Lydia ran upstairs to her bedroom and flung herself down onto her bed. Everyone seemed so happy.

Even Danny was settling down better than her. He went to a different school from hers so she didn't even have him to talk to at breaktimes.

The school cup . . . Had she made the right decision? At that moment it didn't feel like it but Lydia suspected that, no matter what she had done, she would have felt the same way. So much for letting her conscience decide! All Lydia wanted to do now was hide. Hide under the duvet and never come out again.

Ever.

Three

I Don't Have It

'I wish they'd get on with it. We've been standing here for ages,' Frankie moaned. She shifted her weight from her right to her left foot. Lydia nodded but said nothing. 'You're very quiet,' Frankie whispered.

'Am I?' Lydia forced a smile. The assembly hall was now completely different from the way it had been the previous afternoon. It was filled to overflowing with the rest of the school, all whispering and coughing. Lydia looked around. There, two rows in front of her, was Anne. A slight smile played over Anne's face. As Lydia watched, Anne turned to look at the cup cabinet, then back at Lydia. Lydia turned her head to look at the cabinet but there were too many heads in the way for her to see more than the top left-hand corner of it.

'Attention everyone. Pay attention,' Mr Simmers, the headmaster, called out from up on the stage.

Mr Simmers was a stout man who obviously enjoyed his food. He wore round spectacles which were too small for his face and made him look like a wise owl. Lydia liked him though. On her first day at Collivale, he had gone out of his way to be friendly. He did rather talk as if he'd just swallowed a dictionary but at least he always seemed to have a smile on his face. Except for now.

'I have something very serious to report,' Mr Simmers said. He peered over the top of his glasses, his beady gaze darting across the assembly hall, lighting on person after person. 'The Collivale best all-rounder's sports cup has been stolen.'

An audible gasp filled the hall. Lydia's mouth dropped open. She looked across at Anne but Anne was looking straight up at the stage.

'Who'd fleece that dusty old piece of tin foil!' Frankie scoffed.

Lydia had to fight to breathe normally. All at once, she was burning up.

'Now, as it was only that cup and no other which was taken, I'm inclined to believe that it was the work of someone from this school, rather than a professional thief. BUT I WANT IT BACK.' Mr Simmers' cheeks puffed out as he spoke. 'If the perpetrator of this . . . this perfidious act owns up to his or her transgression immediately after assembly, then they will not be dealt with *too* severely. If, however, they do *not* own up and I find out who it is . . .' Mr Simmers left the unfinished sentence dangling ominously in the air. Not a sound could be heard. Not a murmur, not a whisper.

Without warning one of the assembly hall doors was flung open. Everyone jumped. Lydia, along with everyone else, turned to see what was happening. Mrs Irving, the history teacher, entered the hall and took a quick look around before almost running up the stage steps. Lydia's stomach churned. She chewed nervously on her bottom lip as she watched Mrs Irving whisper in Mr Simmers' ear. Mr Simmers scanned the hall as if he had suddenly developed X-ray vision.

Trembling, Lydia glanced across to the cup cabinet again before returning her gaze to the stage. Mrs Irving was off the stage now and heading for the door.

'Could Julie Morgan, repeat Julie Morgan of class 4B, please report to the school secretary immediately after assembly. Thank you.' The school secretary's voice rang out over the school's public announcement system, making Lydia jump.

'Frankie, I'm . . .' Lydia began.

'Assembly dismissed.' Mr Simmers' icy voice effectively halted Lydia's words.

'Frankie, I need to talk to you,' Lydia whispered.

She turned with the rest of her row and they all

stood, waiting for their turn to troop out of the hall.

'What about?' Frankie asked, turning her head to face Lydia.

'Would Lydia Henson please stay behind.'

It was an order, not a request. The headmaster's words stopped all whispers in the hall. Lydia was suddenly drowning under the weight of the speculative stares of those around her. She felt totally sick. She looked around dismayed, then across the hall to where Mr Simmers stood. Why had he asked her to stay behind? What was going on? Lydia tried to catch Anne's eye, but Anne looked straight ahead as she waited for her row to be allowed to leave the hall.

'I'll see you later, Lydia,' Frankie frowned, puzzled.

Lydia waited for the rest of the school to amble out. She kept her head bent, unable to meet the curious glances directed at her. Then she moved slowly down to the front of the hall. Mr Simmers stood on the stage, towering over her like a New York skyscraper next to a beetle. He glowered at Lydia until his heavy, bushy eyebrows met over his nose. His lips pursed in an intense frown, he walked over to the side of the stage and marched down the steps.

'Do you have something you wish to tell me, Lydia?' he asked.

Lydia's 'No, sir' was stuck somewhere between

her tongue and the roof of her mouth. She shook her head slowly.

'Follow me,' Mr Simmers commanded.

The headmaster strode out of the hall, not bothering to look at Lydia. Lydia followed him – she could do nothing else. Why had he picked her out? If only Lydia could have spoken to Anne – just for a minute. She longed to know what was going on but who could she ask? Certainly not Mr Simmers. He looked as if his head was about to explode. Maybe he knew about her being in the hall late the previous afternoon after school. Maybe Old Baldie had told him and Mr Simmers just wanted to talk to her about who else she might have seen around at the same time.

To Lydia's surprise, Mr Simmers didn't lead the way to his office but instead turned right. Lydia wondered where they were going. She didn't have to wait long to find out. The girls' cloakroom. Lydia had to trot to keep up with Mr Simmers' long stride. Once inside, they turned down the second aisle to the left of the cloakroom doors and Lydia saw Mrs Irving and Mr Balding the caretaker ahead. The cloakroom was almost steaming with warm, damp coats hanging on coat hooks up and down its aisles. At last Mr Simmers came to an abrupt halt.

The headmaster and Mr Balding looked at each other. Mr Balding nodded almost imperceptibly.

'Lydia Henson, is this your locker?' Mr

Simmers pointed to the locker in front of him but his eyes never left Lydia's face.

Lydia tried to speak but the words got lost in her throat. She swallowed, then tried again.

'Yes, sir.' The words came out as a frightened squeal.

'Open it,' Mr Simmers ordered.

Lydia looked at all three of the grown-ups before looking at her locker. They all looked poised, as if one false move on her part and they would pounce, tearing her to pieces. Lydia's heart pummelled her ribs. What was wrong? What was going on?

Wiping her clammy hands on her skirt, she walked forward. She reached out to the combination lock on her locker door before realizing that the locker door was shut but not locked.

'It's open,' she said, surprised.

'Mr Balding has been opening all the lockers in here and in the boys' cloakroom on my instructions,' said Mr Simmers. 'I had reason to believe that the sports cup would still be on the school premises.'

Lydia stared from her locker to Mr Simmers' stony face and back again. Her eyes widened to their absolute limits.

'I don't have it. I don't have the cup,' she said, aghast.

'Open your locker, Lydia,' Mr Simmers repeated grimly.

Lydia slowly reached out for the door handle. It was cool beneath her fingertips. She swallowed hard. She could hear Mr Balding wheezing in the background. The sound came from far away. She had to strain to hear it. Immediately around her was silence. A sudden sound, like bucketfuls of gravel being thrown onto the flat roof of the girls' cloakroom, made Lydia jump. Outside, the rain, which had been bad enough before, was now tipping down. A smell like damp towels came from all the coats. Lydia's mouth was dry. Her palms were clammy. She grasped the locker handle and pulled it open. A glint of silver dazzled her. It took a few moments for Lydia to focus. And there, in front of her PE kit and her scarf and gloves – was the sports cup.

Four

Believe Me

'I didn't put it there, sir. I don't know how it got there,' Lydia said, astounded.

'Lydia, I'm deeply disappointed in you,' said Mr Simmers, shaking his head.

'But I didn't do it. I didn't steal the sports cup. You've got to believe me . . .'

'Then what's it doing in your locker?'

'I . . . I don't know, sir.'

Mr Simmers shook his head again. 'Thank you Mrs Irving, Mr Balding. That will be all.'

The caretaker and the history teacher each gave Lydia a grim look before walking past her without saying a word.

'I didn't take the cup, sir. I swear I didn't,' Lydia said again.

'Have you told the combination number of your locker to anyone else?' asked Mr Simmers.

Reluctantly, Lydia shook her head. If only she had!

'Mr Balding tells me that no-one else had this

locker before you,' said Mr Simmers. 'Could someone else have memorized the number while you were opening it?'

Lydia racked her brains. She always cupped her left hand over her right when she was opening her locker just so that no-one would see her number.

'I don't think so, sir,' she whispered at last.

'Then I fail to see how the cup could have got into your locker, if you didn't put it there and no-one else *could* have put it there. All the locker combination numbers are unique and Mr Balding keeps the list of numbers locked up at all times.' Mr Simmers frowned. 'If this was some kind of foolish prank, Lydia, then I have to tell you, I'm *not* amused. Now I don't believe you meant to really steal it, otherwise you could have taken it home with you. Certainly you'd have taken it off the school premises. As yet, I fail to grasp your motivation for removing the cup but I intend to make an example of you. I won't tolerate such behaviour.'

'But I didn't do it, sir. You've got to believe me . . .'

'Lydia,' Mr Simmers said quietly. 'Mr Balding has informed me that he saw you in the assembly hall last night after school. He didn't know your name but he recognized you when I brought you into the cloakroom.'

Lydia swallowed hard. That explained the look that had passed between them.

'Were you in the assembly hall last night?' Mr Simmers asked.

Lydia could feel herself shaking. She felt as if she was tipping over, as if the ground was disappearing out from under her feet.

Tell him. Tell him about Anne hiding by the stage in the hall. You weren't alone. *Tell him* . . .

But Lydia didn't want to get Anne into trouble as well. Besides, what good would it do? Nothing could change the fact that the cup had been found in her locker . . .

'I didn't do it.'

'Lydia, did you take the cup?'

'No, sir, I never touched it.'

'You'd swear to that?'

'I . . . I . . .' Lydia couldn't say any more. She *had* touched it. Last evening, she had reached out her hand and touched it. That image kept spinning around in her head.

'There's a very easy way to clear all this up. I can call in the police and have the cup checked for your fingerprints,' said Mr Simmers grimly.

Lydia trembled violently. Her mouth filled with saliva. She swallowed over and over to stop herself from throwing up all over her shoes. *The police* . . .

'Should I do that, Lydia?' Mr Simmers asked. A small pulse throbbed in his cheek. Lydia watched it, mesmerized.

'Answer me!'

Lydia jumped. Slowly, oh so slowly, she shook her head.

'But I didn't *take* it.' Even to Lydia's ears, her voice sounded weak and unconvincing. Lydia tried again. 'I DIDN'T TAKE IT.'

'Which class do you have now?' Mr Simmers sighed.

'Double English with Mr Fine,' Lydia replied, her voice quivering. Her throat and eyes felt as if they were full of shards of broken glass.

'He's your class teacher, isn't he?' Mr Simmers asked. Lydia nodded. 'I'll take you back to your class,' Mr Simmers continued. 'You're to come and see me at lunchtime. I should have worked out a suitable punishment by then.' He shook his head. 'I would never have thought it of you, Lydia. I thought you were sensible.'

'But that's not fair . . .'

'Lydia, if you didn't take the cup, who did?' asked the headmaster, exasperated.

'I don't know,' Lydia answered miserably.

'Then perhaps you'd like to tell me *why* anyone would want to put the cup in your locker?'

'I don't know that either.'

The headmaster pursed his lips. 'You don't seem to know much, Lydia. Explain to me how the cup found its way into your locker when only you and the caretaker know the combination. Or are you accusing Mr Balding?'

Lydia didn't speak, didn't move. She didn't trust

herself to do either. She wanted to scream. She wanted to run out of the cloakroom and out of the school and keep running.

'If you knew the answer to just one of my questions, I might be more inclined to believe your pleas of innocence,' said Mr Simmers.

Lydia's mind whirled as they walked back to her classroom. How had the sports cup got into her locker? She hadn't put it there. She'd chickened out of stealing it at the last minute – just as Anne had said she would.

So how had it got there?

It was too much of a coincidence that she'd been talking to Anne about taking it and then it'd turned up in her locker.

Which meant only one thing.

Somehow Anne was involved. But how had Anne known the combination number to her locker? And why would she do such a thing? But it had to be Anne. Who else could it be? Slowly, Lydia shook her head.

I'm letting my imagination run riot and it's just a coincidence, she decided wretchedly.

The whole thing was so confusing. Why would Anne – or anyone else for that matter – want to get her into trouble?

Mr Simmers and Lydia entered her class, just as Mr Fine was pleading with Frankie.

'Frances, could you please come up here and make this rotten VCR work! You have the knack! I don't!' Mr Fine looked that close to kicking the stand that held the VCR and the TV across the room!

Frankie raised her eyes heavenwards and stood up. Lydia recognized that look. Every time Mr Fine used the VCR, it was always the same thing. Frankie always ended up having to operate it or fix it because the teacher didn't have a clue.

When Frankie saw Lydia and Mr Simmers however, she sat down again.

'Ah, Mr Fine, a word. Lydia, return to your seat.'

Mr Simmers and Mr Fine stood with their backs to the class. Lydia was unable to hear what they were saying but she heard her name being repeated over and over. She sat down next to Frankie, who frowned at her but said nothing. Lydia sat at her desk and got out her English workbook. She opened it. The words swam in front of her. She didn't want to look at anyone or talk to anyone. She needed to be by herself, to think.

Seconds later she heard, 'Is it true you tried to swipe our sports cup?'

Lydia quickly raised her head from her book. Shaun, who sat in front of her, had an accusing look on his face.

'Keep your voice down,' Lydia pleaded.

'Well? Did you try and fleece our sports cup or

not?' Shaun repeated at the top of his voice.

Lydia's face burned like white-hot fire as she felt all eyes in the classroom on her.

'Shaun Lucas, be quiet!' Mr Fine glared at him before turning back to the headmaster.

'I . . . I never . . . d-did,' Lydia stammered.

'Do me a favour! Then what was it doing in your locker?' Shaun scoffed.

Lydia heard Frankie inhale sharply from beside her.

'How did you know it was found there?' Lydia whispered.

'Anne was in the cloakroom getting her pencil-case when you arrived there with Mr Simmers. She heard everything,' Shaun took great delight in telling her.

Lydia glanced over at Anne who sat beside the window. Anne was watching her – a knowing, contemptuous expression on her face.

'I never took that cup. I haven't a clue how it got into my locker,' Lydia protested.

She turned to Frankie, who was reading her English workbook as if it had suddenly become the most riveting thing she'd ever seen.

'Frankie, you believe me, don't you? I never took the sports cup.'

As Lydia watched, Frankie glanced across at Anne before returning to her English workbook without saying a word.

'You've got a nerve. You come up here, steal

our school cup and think you can get away with it?' said Shaun.

Lydia clamped her lips together.

'I didn't reckon you for a – what do you call it down in London? – a tea leaf!' Shaun said maliciously when Lydia didn't speak.

'I am not a thief,' Lydia protested.

'No? How did the cup get into your locker then?' Shaun taunted.

'Leave me alone,' Lydia said fiercely.

She looked across the room at Anne. Anne was grinning at her, a satisfied smirk on her face.

The volume of chatter in the class had risen now. Her whole body burning up, Lydia knew they were all talking about her.

'That's quite enough noise.' Mr Fine turned back to his class, his brown-black eyes glinting with annoyance. 'And if I have to tell you again, Shaun, you will spend the rest of this double lesson standing in the corner of the room.'

'Tea leaf!' Shaun directed one last salvo before turning to face the front again.

'Thank you, Mr Simmers. I'll make sure it gets done,' Mr Fine said.

Lydia glanced up from her book to see Mr Simmers watching her. She quickly glanced down again, listening as the headmaster left the classroom. Her face was on fire. But why? She'd done nothing wrong. So why did she feel so guilty? Because she'd touched the cup. She'd actually touched it. And she'd come so close to taking it . . .

At the sound of the closing door, the class was unusually quiet.

'That's more like it,' Mr Fine said. 'Now let's keep it that way for the rest of the morning. Take out your English workbooks. Exercise fifteen.'

'Frankie, I need to talk to you,' Lydia said as quietly as she could. 'I need your help.'

Frankie didn't look at her. Lydia shook Frankie's forearm under the desk.

'Frankie, I didn't steal the sports cup. I swear I didn't,' Lydia whispered.

Still Frankie didn't look at her.

'Don't you believe me?' Lydia asked desperately. 'Please, Frankie, I need to talk to you. It's about the Cosmics and what Anne said to me about . . .'

'Lydia Henson, don't you think you're in enough trouble without adding to it?' Mr Fine appeared from nowhere to stand before her desk.

Lydia looked around. Everyone was watching her. And Lydia knew that they all thought she was guilty. Even Frankie didn't believe her. Lydia couldn't stand any more. Her eyes stung with unshed, unwelcome tears. All at once her cheeks were wet and Lydia knew she was crying.

'Sir, can I go to the toilet, please?' Lydia whispered.

Mr Fine frowned down at her. 'Go on, then. But hurry up.'

Lydia stood up and walked slowly to the door, her head bent so that no-one could see her face, so that no-one would catch her eye. Her hand had just reached the door handle when behind her, very softly, very simply, someone called out, 'Thief!'

'Shaun Lucas! Up here – now!' Mr Fine ordered furiously.

Lydia left the classroom, closing the door quietly behind her.

Five

Tell The Truth

'Danny, go to your room,' said Dad.

'Why?'

'Because we said so,' said Mum.

Danny looked around the table, taking in the stony expressions on his mum's and dad's faces and the sombre expression on his sister's face.

'Is Lydia in trouble?' he asked gleefully.

'Danny, I don't want to have to tell you again,' Dad said softly.

'All right, all right, I'm going,' Danny grumbled as he left the room. 'Why do I always have to miss the good bits? It's not fair . . .'

Lydia watched as her mum stood up and went to close the living-room door firmly behind Danny.

Here it comes, Lydia thought bitterly.

She knew that Mr Simmers had phoned her mum and dad and told them about the sports cup being found in her locker. Lydia wished she'd been a fly on the wall when the headmaster had spoken to her parents. What had he said? How had he put it? And most importantly – how had Mum and Dad taken it? She was about to find out.

Lydia glanced up at her parents. They were watching her. She immediately lowered her eyes.

Don't do that. They'll think you're guilty if you do that . . .

Lydia looked up. The silence in the room weighed down on her like concrete blocks on her chest. She tried to speak but her tongue was so dry it was stuck to the roof of her mouth. Just when Lydia thought she'd scream if the silence lasted any longer, her mum broke it.

'We know you didn't do it,' said Mum. 'I told your headmaster that it was ridiculous.'

'You did?' Lydia's eyes were as round as dinner plates.

'But how did that sports cup get into your locker?' Dad asked. 'Tell the truth.'

Lydia turned to him. 'I don't know.' She shook her head. 'I wish I did.'

'Maybe the thief was disturbed and just put it in the first available locker which happened to be yours?' Dad suggested.

Lydia shook her head. 'I always keep my locker locked.'

'Then it must have been deliberate. Someone must have it in for you,' said Mum.

'Don't talk nonsense,' Dad chided. 'Why would anyone do that to Lydia?'

'That sports cup didn't just walk into her locker. Someone put it there. Some spiteful, vicious person who wanted to see Lydia get into trouble,' Mum snapped back.

'Next you'll be telling me that it's the same person who shot President John Kennedy,' Dad said scornfully.

'I didn't say it was a major school conspiracy. All I meant was . . .'

'All you meant was that the CIA or the FBI or the BBC or the RSPCA have it in for our daughter,' said Dad.

'Well, if you're not going to take this seriously . . .' Mum sniffed.

'You're wrong. I *am* taking this seriously,' Dad said icily.

Dismayed, Lydia watched the anger and frustration being batted back and forth between her parents. Mum and Dad, who usually only argued about who would get which section of the Sunday papers first, were quarrelling with each other.

'So what are we going to do?' Mum asked Dad.

'I don't see that there's much we can do. To think that my little girl . . .'

'I want to go to another school.' The words fell out of Lydia's mouth before she realized what she was saying.

Dad's eyes narrowed. 'Why? Did you do it?'

Lydia stared at her father, shocked.

'Ben, what a thing to say.' Mum sounded as shocked as Lydia.

'I didn't mean it that way,' said Dad impatiently. 'But if she didn't do it, why does she want to run away?'

'Lydia has no intention of running anywhere,' said Mum through thinned lips.

'I don't believe Lydia stole the cup for one second, but we can't get away from the fact that the cup was found in her locker.'

'Who can get away from the fact when you keep dwelling on it like that?' Mum said bitterly.

'I just don't like the idea of anyone thinking that my daughter is a thief.'

'No-one in their right mind would think that . . .'

How could two people agree with each other, yet still argue about it? But that was exactly what Lydia's mum and dad were doing. It was like watching a tennis match. Why? Where? How? Who? Back and forth, back and forth. And all the time, one word kept playing over and over in Lydia's mind as she watched. *THIEF* . . . Lydia put her hands over her ears to stop her head from bursting.

'Stop it!' she screamed. 'Stop talking about me as if I wasn't here. I didn't take the rotten, stupid cup. I didn't. I *didn't*.'

Lydia looked from her dad to her mum and back

again. Mum's eyes flashed like lightning, her lips a hard slash across her face. Whereas Dad . . . Dad had a questioning look in his eyes that he couldn't hide. He didn't think for a moment that Lydia had stolen the cup, *but* . . . Lydia could see the 'but' written all over his face.

Mum's angry. And Dad . . . Dad doesn't know what to think, Lydia realized sadly.

Strange, but Lydia had been sure it'd be the other way around.

'Lydia, what were you doing alone in the assembly hall after school on the night the cup was taken?' Lydia's mum asked.

'I was . . . I wasn't alone, Mum. Anne Turner was with me – only the caretaker didn't see her.'

'You *weren't* alone?' Dad turned quickly. 'Why didn't you tell that to Mr Simmers?'

'Because I didn't want to get Anne into trouble as well,' Lydia replied.

And that was the truth, but what good did it do her? Lydia could still remember Anne's malicious smirk in the classroom earlier. And Anne was the one who'd told everyone about the cup being found in Lydia's locker. Understanding burnt through Lydia as she realized that Anne didn't like her much, that Anne had never liked her much. But why? *Why?*

'Lydia, it's not a question of getting Anne in trouble as well,' Dad frowned. 'She can tell the headmaster that you didn't do it.'

Lydia shook her head. 'Anne left the school before me,' she admitted.

Silence.

'Why on earth were the two of you hanging around after school?' Dad asked, furiously.

Lydia chewed on her bottom lip but didn't answer. Any explanation now would just make her look even more guilty. What was she supposed to say?

I was going to take the cup so I could join the Cosmics, but I chickened out. I touched it, but I didn't take it. It's got my fingerprints on it, but I'm innocent . . .

Yeah, right!

'Anne and I . . . We were just talking. If I tell Mr Simmers about Anne now, it'll look like I'm just trying to pin the blame on her,' Lydia replied at last. 'And it wouldn't do any good anyway – she couldn't know my locker combination.'

No-one said a word.

'Dad, Mum, please let me go to another school,' Lydia begged.

'Lydia, you are going to stay at Collivale School and you're not going to bow your head or look away from anyone. You have nothing to be ashamed of,' Mum said stonily.

'It's not that simple, Mum.'

'Oh, yes it is,' Mum argued. 'If you walk around with your chin on the pavement and skulk in corners at the first sign of anyone you know, everyone will think you're too afraid to face them. D'you understand?'

'Yes, Mum,' Lydia whispered.

Only Lydia knew it really wasn't that simple. What about earlier at school, when Shaun Lucas had called her a thief in front of the whole class? Lydia knew she wasn't a thief. No way was she a thief. So why had she spent the next half-hour crying in the toilets?

Dad stood up and walked over to the window. He stared out into the night, his whole body held rigid as if he was in pain. Lydia held her breath. Maybe that way she could hold on to the tears in her eyes. Mum took hold of Lydia's hand and squeezed it gently.

This is it, Lydia thought miserably. This is the worst moment of my life.

She was soon to find out that she was wrong.

Six

It Begins

'Thief! Thief! Thief!'

Lydia's blood roared through her body. Her face was burning; burning hot, then burning cold. And her stomach turned and churned inside her.

I don't care, Lydia thought fiercely. Call me what you like – I don't care.

She stood with her back against the storeroom wall, surrounded on all sides by the others in her class. Her former friends. Every lunchtime for over a week now, Lydia had had to go through exactly the same thing. They all lay in wait – carefully choosing the moment when they could torment her. The moment when the teachers were far enough away so that even if they did see what was going on, they would only be able to make out numbers, not specific faces.

Only the teachers never saw anything and Lydia had given up hoping that they would. And now it was worse. Now it wasn't just the ones in her class tormenting her; people from other classes were beginning to join in too.

'Thief . . . thief . . . thief . . . !' they chanted, over and over.

Shut up . . . shut up . . .

Lydia thought the words were in her head. She thought her mind was screaming them, desperate but silent.

'Shut up . . . SHUT UP!' Lydia opened her mouth to exhale and the words fell out before she could stop them. 'SHUT UP . . .' Her words were petrol thrown onto a bonfire.

'THIEF! THIEF!'

Lydia bit into her bottom lip, hard, until she could taste her own blood in her mouth. She turned her head slowly. They were all there: Anne, Shaun, Kwame, Maxine, Bharti, Frankie . . . Lydia looked directly at her ex-best friend, Frankie. Her eyes narrowed and filled with scalding hate. Frankie didn't chant with the rest of them but she didn't stand up for Lydia either. And, surprisingly, Anne wasn't shouting with the rest of the mob either. She stood next to Frankie, their arms linked as they watched.

Lydia saw Anne say something to Frankie which was lost under the chants of the rest of the crowd. Then Anne and Frankie turned and walked away to another part of the playground.

'THIEF! THIEF!'

The buzzer sounded twice for the second lunch

session. The chanting of the mob trailed away to nothing. Some were already turning away and heading for the canteen. After all, today was fish and chips day! Some of the others looked uncertain, as if they wanted to stay but not by themselves. Laughing and chatting, the rest of the crowd finally turned and ambled off. Lydia watched them walk away from her as if nothing had happened, as if she didn't even exist. The bones in her legs turned to jelly. She slid down the wall and hugged her legs to her, resting her head on her knees. Her whole body was hurting. Each time 'THIEF!' was yelled at her, it hurt worse than a punch in her stomach. And over the last week she'd had to take so many punches.

'I'm not going to cry. I won't let any of you make me cry.' Lydia whispered the words over and over.

It seemed to be working. For once the tears that always seemed to be stinging her eyes these days didn't run down onto her cheeks.

'I'm not going to cry,' Lydia said again.

She forced herself to stand up. It was time for her to go into lunch as well. Lunch was such an ordeal that she'd skipped it for the last couple of days. But not any more.

'I won't give any of you the satisfaction,' she said, trying to convince herself. She took a deep breath and headed for the canteen.

★   ★   ★

Lydia grimaced as soggy, greasy chips were slapped onto her plate. Everyone looked forward to Friday's lunch, but the fish looked as if it had died of old age and the chips were doing the backstroke in a puddle of oil.

'Anything else, pet?' asked the dinner-lady.

Lydia shook her head. She turned, swallowing hard. Now for the hard part. She had to somehow get across the lunch hall without catching anyone's eye. Lydia started forward, her head high, her gaze concentrating on the far wall. But that wasn't the worst part. Not by any means. It was listening to the silence spreading before her as she approached each table. Then as she passed, the whispers and the laughter started, growing louder and louder as she got further away.

That was the worst part.

Lydia sat down at a table by herself. She pronged a chip with her fork and began to chew. It was like eating with a really bad head cold. The chips grated down the back of her throat as she swallowed and Lydia couldn't taste a thing.

'Bharti, sit down and be quiet.'

At the sound of Mrs Binchy's angry voice, Lydia looked up. The teacher stood glaring at Bharti, who held her lunch plate in her hand. From the pinched look on Mrs Binchy's face, she was obviously at the end of her tether. Lydia recognized Bharti, who was in the same year as her but not in the same class. Bharti had also been at one of the Cosmic meetings Lydia had attended but they hadn't said that much to each other. Mind you, that was before Anne had decided that Bharti didn't belong and had thrown her out of the group.

'I can't sit with her.' Bharti pointed to Lydia. 'My mum said I mustn't talk to her 'cause she steals things.'

'SIT DOWN!' Mrs Binchy roared.

Bharti sat down quickly.

'Bharti, you will sit there and eat your lunch without another word. I've had just about enough of you for one day.' And with that Mrs Binchy strode off.

Lydia returned her attention to her plate, viciously pronging another chip. Head bent, she swallowed hard over and over again, waiting for the lump in her throat to deflate. At the moment it was the size of Jupiter. A burning sensation on the top of her head told Lydia that Bharti was watching her. Gritting her teeth, Lydia looked up suddenly.

'What're you looking at?' she snapped.

'My mum said I wasn't to talk to you, but I never take any notice of what my mum says,' said Bharti. A moment's silence followed. 'Did you steal the sports cup?'

Lydia shook her head.

'I didn't think you did.' Bharti shrugged.

'Why not? Everyone else does,' Lydia said bitterly.

Bharti shrugged again. 'I never do what I'm supposed to. That's why I'm always in trouble.'

Over Bharti's shoulder, Lydia saw Anne and Frankie walk through the door, arm in arm. They both noticed Lydia immediately. Anne said something to Frankie, who tilted back her head and roared with laughter. Lydia looked away, her face on fire.

'Hhmm! I bet Anne's happy now,' said Bharti as she watched them too.

'What d'you mean?' Lydia asked.

'She and Frankie used to be best friends until you turned up. Then it was you and Frankie,' Bharti explained. 'Now it's back to the status quo.'

'I didn't know that,' Lydia said thoughtfully.

'Now you do,' said Bharti.

Lydia turned to look at Anne and Frankie again, watching as they laughed at some unknown joke. And in that moment Lydia knew beyond a shadow of a doubt that Anne was the one who'd set her up.

Seven

The Message Spreads

'Mum, I don't want to go.'

'I can't manage the shopping all by myself.'

'Danny's going with you,' Lydia protested. 'Why d'you need me as well?'

'Lydia, I've had enough of this. Go and put your coat on. And wear your trainers or your boots – it's slippery outside.'

Lydia scowled up at her mum. She recognized that tone of voice. Her mum had made up her mind and nothing short of a ton of dynamite would shift her now. Lydia turned her head to stare back out of the window. The road and pavement glistened like glass from the severe overnight frost. High above, grey clouds were beginning to sweep across the town. Lydia sighed. All she wanted to do was watch the world go by from the front room window. Why couldn't everyone just leave her alone?

'Lydia, move! NOW!' Mum said angrily.

'But someone from my class might see me,' Lydia whispered.

'So what? You didn't do anything to be ashamed of,' Mum said. 'How many times must I tell you? Hold your head high and don't let anyone make you feel ashamed of something you haven't done.'

Lydia sighed deeply as she uncurled her legs from beneath her and stood up. She looked at her mum again, making a silent appeal.

'Hurry up, Lydia. I don't want to spend my entire Saturday stuck in the supermarket,' Mum said.

So much for that! Lydia looked down at Danny, who lay flat out on his stomach in front of the television. He was playing with his latest video game.

'Danny, go and put your shoes on. You can't go shopping in your slippers,' Mum said.

Danny pressed the pause button. 'Can't I just finish . . . ?'

'No, you can't!' Mum exploded. 'You children are driving me up the wall and on to the roof! Now I want both of you in the car in *one* minute.'

And with that Mum marched out of the room.

'Since last week, everyone's been so grouchy,' Danny complained. 'Snap! Snap! Snap! All the time.'

'And it's all my fault. Go on! Say it!' Lydia said furiously.

'Well, excuse me all over the place! That's not what I meant and you know it. Don't you snap at me as well.'

'Sorry, Danny.' Lydia dragged the words out.

'I should think so, too.' Danny sniffed. 'I don't care what anyone else says, Lyddy. I know you didn't do anything wrong.'

Lydia smiled. Before Danny realized what she had planned, she kissed him on the cheek.

'Ugh! Yeuk!' Danny rubbed his cheek vigorously. 'I'm going to have a whole load of spots there tomorrow! Are you nuts?'

'I must be to kiss my baby brother,' Lydia said sourly.

Danny and Lydia glared at each other until their lips started to twitch. Then they both started laughing. Lydia pushed lightly against Danny's left shoulder. Danny pushed her back. They both smiled.

'Come on. We'd better get going before Mum goes into orbit,' said Lydia.

After putting on their trainers, coats, scarves, hats and gloves, they both left the house in silence.

Lydia emerged from the car like a snail from its shell. She looked around, her teeth clamped together so tightly that her jaw ached. The car-park was almost full, with people milling around everywhere. The supermarket was at the edge of town, very close to the moors. Thanks to the traffic, it had taken them ages to get there – at least fifteen minutes – but Lydia wished fervently that the journey could have lasted until everything was closed. The supermarket was usually only six or seven minutes' drive from the house and Lydia's mum wasn't exactly a Sunday driver. According to Dad she was more of a speed demon! And ever since she and Dad had bought their brand new car a couple of months before, there'd been no stopping her!

Lydia looked out beyond the car-park to the moors. Although dull grey clouds filled the sky above the Tarwich shops and houses, the sky over the moors blazed pink and orange. These colours moved around each other in a slow, fluid dance. Lydia felt a peculiar prickling sensation at the back of her neck. She rubbed her nape as she stared at the strange sky. She felt oddly attracted to the sight and yet, at the same time, it gave her a queasy feeling in the pit of her stomach. Someone laughing nearby brought Lydia out of her daydream. She hastily looked down.

Don't let me see anyone from school. *Please*.

Maybe, if she said it enough times, it would come true.

'Another fun-packed Saturday getting crushed at Sainsbury's,' Mum grumbled.

Moments later, she passed the food trolley to Lydia and they all entered the supermarket.

'Danny, just behave yourself, OK. I don't

want any of your nonsense today,' Mum said.

'But I haven't done anything,' Danny protested.

'Let's just keep it that way, shall we?' Mum said.

'Is that fair or what?' Danny huffed. 'I'm being told off and I haven't even done anything.'

Danny muttered under his breath for at least an aisle and a half. For the first couple of aisles, Lydia hardly dared to look up. Everyone would be looking at her. They would all know what she was supposed to have done.

Don't look up, Lydia. Then you won't have to face anyone. You won't have to see that word in everyone's eyes, on everyone's faces. *Thief* . . .

'Lyddy, have you got a headache? Is the light hurting your eyes?' Danny whispered.

'No. Why?'

'You keep looking down,' Danny said.

'Shut up and leave me alone,' Lydia hissed.

They turned down the third aisle – full of slices of bloody beef and chilled lamb and cooked chickens, all wrapped in polystyrene and cellophane. And then Lydia saw her. Anne. With her mum.

The only sound in the whole of the supermarket was Lydia's blood roaring through her body. She stared, horror-stricken. It took a few moments for Anne to realize that she was being watched. Her head turned and her eyes met Lydia's. As Lydia watched, Anne's eyes narrowed and a tiny smile played over her lips. Lydia lowered her head immediately, every atom of her body on fire.

'Mum, I don't feel well. Can I go and sit in the car?' Lydia whispered.

With a frown, Mum placed a hand on Lydia's forehead.

'You don't have a temperature,' she said.

'I feel terrible. Please.'

'No, I don't think so. Breathing in this recycled air-conditioning is a lot healthier than breathing in carbon monoxide fumes in the car-park,' Mum said firmly.

'Mum, Anne Turner from my class is in front of us. Please let me leave,' Lydia pleaded.

'No. I'd say she's all the more reason to stand your ground,' Mum replied.

And that was the end of that. Lydia had no choice but to keep pushing the trolley. She kept her eyes on her hands in front of her.

'Mum, that's the girl I was telling you about,' Anne said at the top of her voice. 'That's the thief!'

There was no way everyone in the aisle didn't hear Anne. Feeling sick, Lydia looked around. Everyone was looking at her.

Anne's mum pulled her daughter away from Lydia as if she thought that being a supposed thief was contagious.

'Don't you dare call my sister a thief,' Danny said furiously.

His voice was even louder than Anne's. Lydia

wanted to crawl into the nearest hole and never come out again.

'Danny, that's enough,' Mum said quietly.

'But she said . . .'

'I'm well aware of what she said,' Mum interrupted. Mum turned to Anne's mum.

'Mrs Turner, my daughter isn't a thief. I suggest you tell your daughter to get her facts straight,' Mum said, adding under her breath, 'And teach her some manners while you're at it.'

'Anne's told me all about your daughter,' Anne's mum said pointedly. 'That cup has been at Collivale School since I was a girl. She had no right to take it.'

'Lydia didn't take it.' Lydia's mum spoke even more quietly than before. 'In fact, your daughter was with her the night the cup went missing.'

Mrs Turner frowned and turned to Anne. 'Is that true?'

'No, Mum,' Anne replied immediately. 'Lydia's just trying to wriggle off the hook and put me on it instead.'

'That's a lie. You were with me that night,' Lydia gasped.

'No, I wasn't. You're just a liar as well as a thief,' Anne said viciously.

'My daughter is neither of those things,' Lydia's mum denied.

'If you say so,' said Anne's mum. 'Come on, Anne. We have shopping to *buy*.'

'And just what does that mean? Are you insinuating something?' Lydia's mum asked.

'Mum, let's go. Please let's go,' Lydia implored.

The decision to get away was taken out of Lydia's hands. Mrs Turner took Anne firmly by the hand and practically dragged her away. Scalding hot tears burnt a trail down Lydia's cheeks. She looked around. The eyes of everyone in the aisle were on her. The security camera at the end of the aisle, past the checkout counter, was trained on her. The whole world had turned into a pair of eyes.

'Mum, can I sit in the car? *Please?*'

'No.'

'I hate you,' Lydia hissed at her mum. 'I hate you and I'll never forgive you.'

'That's enough, Lydia,' Mum said quietly.

Beside Lydia, Danny started to sniff. Slow, embarrassed tears that he couldn't control slid down his cheeks.

'It's OK, Danny. I'm sorry. Don't cry.' Lydia put her arm around her brother's shoulders.

'I'm not crying.' Danny wiped his eyes with the back of his hand.

They carried on walking down the aisle. Lydia looked at her brother. Even if no-one else did, Danny believed in her. Not in the way that Mum did, by thinking that Lydia should hold her head high and that was all that mattered. Not in the way that Dad did, by believing that no daughter of his could have done such a thing. No, Danny really and truly believed that *she*, Lydia, hadn't stolen the cup. And Lydia needed that – more than anything else.

As they queued at the checkout counter, Lydia smiled tentatively at Danny. He smiled back. They didn't need to do or say anything else.

'Lydia?'

At the sound of her name, Lydia's head whipped around. She couldn't believe it.

'Frankie!' Lydia said, stunned.

'Hello, Lydia.' Frankie smiled uncertainly. 'Er . . . how are you?'

'I'm OK,' Lydia said slowly. Why was Frankie asking? She didn't care. She hadn't said one word to Lydia over the last week. Not one.

'I . . . I just wanted to say . . . I know you didn't take the cup . . .'

'Oh yeah? What's changed your mind, *Frances*?' Lydia asked, her eyes blazing. She'd used Frankie's real name deliberately, wanting to give back just a little of the hurt she was feeling – even if it was just a *very little*.

'Lydia, I'm on your side . . .'

'Are you, Frances? You could've fooled me,' Lydia said, turning away from her.

'Look, can we . . . ?' Frankie got no further.

'Frankie, I didn't know you were here.' Appearing as if from nowhere, Anne linked arms with Frankie, ignoring Lydia and her family completely. 'Come and say hello to my mum.'

Frankie allowed Anne to lead her away. She turned her head to look back at Lydia, frustration written all over her face.

'Lydia, that wasn't very nice,' Mum said quietly.

'What wasn't?'

'Cutting her dead like that. Frankie obviously wanted to talk to you. She was trying to be friendly, which is more than can be said for that other one,' Mum pointed out.

'Well, I didn't want to talk to her.'

'Don't be too proud to let her be your friend,' Mum warned.

'I hate her and Anne and everyone else at that rotten school.'

'Now Lydia . . .'

'I don't want to talk about it,' said Lydia stubbornly.

She wished her mum would just drop the subject. Mum shook her head but took the hint and said nothing.

'I'm your friend, Lyddy,' Danny whispered.

Moments passed before Lydia spoke.

'D'you know something, Danny? In this whole, stinking town you're the only true friend I've got,' she replied.

'Lydia, that's enough. I'm sure you'll find a way of showing everyone that you didn't . . .'

'Don't start that again, Mum,' Lydia interrupted. 'It doesn't matter – not any more.

Danny's the only friend I've got and he's the only friend I want.'

Lydia turned to where Frankie stood with Anne and her mum. Something inside her curled up into a very tight, painful knot and sat like a rock in her stomach. Lydia clenched her fists.

'I'll get my own back on you, Anne, and you, Frankie, if it's the last thing I do. I swear I will,' she said slowly.

And she meant it.

Eight

The Accident

Lydia's mum wheeled the trolley back to the car, followed by Danny and last of all Lydia. They each picked up a carrier bag and started loading up the boot of the car.

'Mum, I want to walk home,' said Lydia when they'd almost finished.

'Why?'

'You're always telling me to get more fresh air and exercise,' Lydia snapped. 'Well, that's what I want to do.'

Mum frowned. 'Fine. You go for your walk – and maybe by the time you get home you'll have walked the devil out of your backside!'

Danny laughed as he always did whenever Mum used that expression. Mum's lips twitched reluctantly.

'As my mother used to say!' she added drily.

It was strange how Mum always quoted Lydia's gran when she was annoyed! The ghost of a smile that flitted across Lydia's face was gone as quickly as it arrived.

'Can I go?' Lydia asked, forcing herself not to snap or snarl or scowl.

'Go on, then,' Mum said. 'Get walking! Just arrive back home in a better mood!'

With a brief nod of gratitude, Lydia headed across the car-park. To get to the car-park exit wasn't the easiest thing in the world. It was uphill all the way.

'Lydia, don't cut across the car-park. Go through the supermarket – it's safer,' Mum called after her.

Lydia shook her head. 'I'll be OK,' she called back. No way did she want to see Anne and Frankie again.

'Mind the cars,' Mum warned.

Lydia nodded and carried on walking.

'I must be crazy!' she muttered to herself.

It would be a long walk home, especially in the freezing cold, but at least it would give her a chance to be alone and think. The car-park was busy with cars coming to and from the super-market but, although Lydia was careful to watch out for approaching cars, she was oblivious to everything else. She had too many other things on her mind.

Think, Lydia – *think*!, she told herself sternly. How had Anne done it? How had Anne set her up?

How would I plant something in someone else's locker? Lydia wondered.

Spy on them while they opened their locker to get the combination? No, that wouldn't work. Anne would need eyes like a hawk to be able to work out Lydia's locker combination from any distance. And if Anne *had* been close enough to see what it was, then Lydia was certain she would've seen her. Unless Anne had used binoculars . . . Lydia stopped walking and frowned. Binoculars! Was that it? Lydia shook her head and carried on walking. Surely someone would've spotted Anne bringing binoculars to school? Besides it was an awful lot of effort to go to just to get someone in trouble. But why not? Maybe Anne reckoned that getting Lydia in trouble and getting Frankie back as her best friend at the same time would be worth the risk.

Lydia's left foot slipped on a patch of ice. She stepped gingerly across it and carried on walking. The sooner she was out of the car-park, and away from Anne and Frankie and everyone else, the better.

That's all I need – to slip and trip and skate along on my bum all the way back down to Sainsbury's, Lydia thought sourly. She smiled slowly. Maybe that wasn't such a bad idea! If she broke an arm or a leg then she'd be off school for a while – as long as she didn't break her neck first! On second thoughts, maybe it wasn't such a good idea after all.

'Lydia, hang on. Didn't you hear me calling you?'

Lydia turned. Frankie came puffing uphill towards her. Lydia glared at her but said nothing. So much for wanting to be alone to walk home and think. She'd only made it as far as the car-park exit! When Frankie reached Lydia, she looked around nervously, then tentatively smiled. Lydia's face remained a frozen mask. Frankie's attempt at a smile faded to nothing.

'I want to talk to you.'

'Why?' asked Lydia. Her voice was icier than the weather. 'So you can rub it in about how Anne set me up?' And I bet you had more than a little to do with it . . . Lydia's eyes narrowed at the thought.

'You know Anne did it?' Frankie asked, astonished.

'I'm not stupid, you know,' Lydia shouted at her. 'I didn't put that stinking cup in my locker. It doesn't take a genius to guess who did.'

'Listen, Lydia. I'm on your side. I want to help you.'

'Yeah, right!' Lydia scoffed.

'I do,' Frankie insisted.

'That's why you told Anne where to go just now in the supermarket – right? That's why you've stood up for me over the past week when everyone's been calling me a . . . calling me names,' said Lydia bitterly.

'I couldn't say anything . . .'

'Of course you couldn't,' Lydia scorned.

'If you'll just listen to me . . .' Frankie put her hand on Lydia's arm.

Lydia slapped it away, pulling back from Frankie at the same time. Frankie's feet slipped on the patch of ice beneath her. Her arms shot out and spun around like a windmill. Then the whole world slowed down into the slowest motion. As Lydia watched horrified, Frankie started falling backwards . . .

Lydia took a step towards her but it was as if she was wading through thick treacle, as if time itself was running so slowly that it was almost at a standstill – except that Lydia could see and understand everything that was happening. Her brain was running at normal speed but her body wasn't. Frankie took a desperate step backwards into the road to steady herself, her arms still flailing. Lydia put out her hand to grab hold of Frankie's coat but her fingers missed it by millimetres. And Frankie carried on falling. Lydia moved forward again to grab for Frankie – but she was too late. The driver of the oncoming car turning into the car-park tried to swerve out of the way, but he couldn't do it in time. The front of his car smacked into Frankie. There was a sickening thud and Frankie spun around like a top before sinking to the ground.

Then time speeded up and everything happened at once.

The screech of brakes, footsteps running, someone screaming, more people shouting – the sounds came from all around. And Lydia stood and stared at Frankie who lay in a crumpled heap in the road.

Do something! DO SOMETHING! The voice in Lydia's head screamed over and over.

'I couldn't help it . . . She came out of nowhere.' The driver of the car stumbled out of his car. He was a tank of a man, easily over two metres high and built like an American footballer. But he stood over Frankie, rocking back and forth, his eyes huge and unblinking. 'She came out of nowhere.' His voice trembled as he spoke. 'It wasn't my fault. She came out of nowhere . . .'

'No! Don't move her. It's dangerous to do that,' said a middle-aged woman who came running up. 'Someone phone for an ambulance.'

'What happened?'

'Get the police . . .'

'Is she badly hurt . . . ?'

The questions, the noise, the people in the car-park – they all faded out to be replaced by the roar of Lydia's blood rushing in her ears.

'You pushed her. I saw you. You pushed her!'

At the sound of Anne's voice, Lydia spun around. With slow dawning shock she realized that Anne was pointing to her.

'Lydia pushed her. I saw it. She and Frankie

were arguing. I ran over here to help and Lydia's hand went out. She pushed her!' screamed Anne.

Lydia gasped as if she'd been kicked in the stomach. She couldn't have said a word if her very life had depended on it. Her tongue was frozen in her mouth. In fact her whole body had gone numb.

'She pushed her. I saw it!' Anne was still pointing at her, hatred blazing on her face.

'I . . . didn't . . .' Lydia's voice was an almost nonexistent whisper. 'I was trying to grab her, to stop her from falling.'

She looked around. Those people who weren't attending to Frankie were watching her, without saying a word. Lydia closed her eyes. She was back in the playground surrounded by the others in her year who watched her and called her names. She opened her eyes again. Grown-ups were all around her, surrounding her and silently watching.

'Lydia, what's going on?' Lydia's mum came running up. Then she saw Frankie lying in the road, still as a grave.

'Oh my God . . .' Lydia's mum breathed.

'I didn't do it, Mum,' Lydia exclaimed desperately. 'It was an accident. She . . .'

Before Lydia could say another word, sirens sounded in the distance, getting closer and closer.

'Mum . . .'

'Shush.' Mum came and stood beside her, as did Danny.

72

'She came out of nowhere . . .' The driver of the car was still staring at Frankie, who hadn't moved a millimetre since she'd been hit.

The ambulance arrived within moments.

'Could you all stand back please,' said a paramedic, trying to push his way through the crowd.

Everyone moved out of his way. Once through, the paramedic immediately crouched down beside Frankie. He and the ambulance woman who'd been driving the ambulance listened as Anne's mother told them what had happened – even though she'd only just arrived herself.

'Her name is Frances Weldon. She goes to school with my daughter. That man over there knocked her over but it was an accident.'

'I . . . I . . .' The driver's skin was like tracing paper now.

'I'll look after him,' the ambulance woman told her colleague. She went over to the driver and linked his arm with her own.

'Come on, sir. Let's get you to the hospital,' she said softly, leading the way to the ambulance.

'Mum, what's wrong with him?' Danny whispered.

'He's in shock,' Mum replied grimly.

Lydia's heart was lodged somewhere in her throat, slowly choking her as the paramedic carefully examined Frankie. A pain in her chest grew sharper and more intense until, with a start, she realized that she had been holding her breath. She expelled the air in her lungs a tiny bit at a time.

'Is Frankie OK?' Anne's mum asked the paramedic.

'I don't know. We'll know more once we've got her to hospital,' the paramedic replied. 'Could you follow us, so we can get some details and contact her parents?'

His colleague came back and helped him to carry Frankie's prone body into the ambulance on a stretcher.

Lydia didn't take her eyes off Frankie. Even when the ambulance doors were shut behind her, Lydia still couldn't look away.

'I saw what you did – and you're not going to get away with it.' Anne's voice rang out loud and clear like a bell.

Lydia turned her head. Anne stood in front of her mother, each of them a mirror of the other.

'I feel sorry for you, Anne Turner. Have you really got nothing better to do than pick on my daughter?' Lydia's mum fumed.

'Come on, Anne. We need to get to the hospital.' Anne's mum took her daughter firmly by the hand and led her quickly away. The crowd around them began to disperse.

Lydia, her mum and Danny all stood stock still, watching everyone else walk away from them.

'Lydia, what happened?' Lydia's mum was still watching the crowd meander back to their cars and the supermarket.

'Nothing,' Lydia mumbled.

'But that's not true, is it?' said Lydia's mum, looking at her for the first time. 'If it was, Frankie wouldn't be on her way to the hospital now.'

'I didn't do that,' Lydia said, aghast.

'I never said you did. I never even *thought* that. But I'd like to know what happened.'

'I . . . Frankie wanted . . . she wanted to talk to me, but . . . I didn't want to talk to her. She . . . she slipped on some ice and fell in front of the car,' Lydia said.

'Ice?'

'There's ice here, Mum.' Danny tentatively slid his trainer along a patch of ice on the ground.

'So why is Anne accusing you of pushing her?' asked Lydia's mum, looking from Danny's foot to Lydia.

'Because she's a real skunk,' Lydia replied bitterly.

'That's enough, Lydia,' her mum said sternly. 'Tell me why Anne is saying that you deliberately hurt Frankie.'

'I didn't push Frankie. I was reaching out my hand to try and stop her from falling,' Lydia said miserably. 'Frankie knows I didn't push her.'

'Frankie's unconscious,' Lydia's mum pointed out.

And Lydia had no answer to that.

'Mum, can we go home now?' Danny asked.

Mum sighed. 'Yes, I think we'd better.'

'Can't we go to the hospital?' asked Lydia.

'I don't think that would be a good idea,' said Lydia's mum. 'I'll phone the hospital later from home to find out how Frankie's doing.'

'But . . .'

'No buts, Lydia. I think we've all had more than enough for one day. It's going to be a nightmare on wheels as it is, trying to get out of this car-park with one of the exits blocked.' Mum looked down at Lydia. 'Frankie will be all right. I'm sure she will,' she added softly.

Lydia didn't answer. She couldn't.

Without another word, Lydia's mum led the way back to the car. Lydia didn't see the car-park, nor the people looking and pointing at her. All she could see was Frankie falling backwards and being hit by the car and spinning around and around and around. She closed her eyes, but it didn't help. The image was even clearer then.

'I hate Tarwich. I wish we'd never come here. I wish we'd never even heard of it,' Danny said quietly once they were in the car.

Mum turned to look at him. 'I'm beginning to feel the same way,' she said.

Lydia leaned her head against the window. That was it then . . . She'd felt that somehow, if everything else continued as normal, then maybe some of it would rub off on her. Her life would get back to normal, too. But now for the first time she realized that it wasn't just her life that was being messed up. She was ruining the lives of her whole family. And in that moment the despair Lydia felt tightened into a knot around the last smidgen of hope left inside her. A knot so tight that any hope left within her was strangled. It didn't matter what happened now. Things would never get back to normal. Ever.

Nine

The Getaway

'Mrs Henson?'

'Yes?'

Lydia and Danny poked their heads around the living-room door. They'd arrived home about three hours ago and barely ten sentences had passed between them since. Lydia couldn't get Frankie out of her mind. Each time she thought things couldn't get any worse, they did.

'My name is Carl Williamson. I'm from the *Tarwich Mercury*.' A short but stout man with slicked-back black hair, pointy teeth like a shark and a smile like a cobra grinned from the front step.

Lydia came out into the hall as her mum placed herself firmly in the doorway between the reporter and her family.

'Can I help you?' Lydia's mum asked coldly.

'I understand your daughter can tell me about the accident her classmate Frances Weldon had. The accident which led to Frances being rushed to hospital.' Carl Williamson was still smiling – an oily, malicious smile.

'Is she all right? D'you know?' Lydia asked from behind her mother.

'Lydia, go back into the living-room,' her mum said urgently.

'Lydia? Are you sorry your friend was knocked unconscious?' Carl was already making notes in his spiral-bound notepad.

Lydia nodded. Of course she was sorry – what kind of question was that?

'Then why did you push Frances in front of the car?' asked the reporter.

Lydia gasped. She stared at him, unable to speak. Something warm and wet ran down her face and over her mouth. Salty tears trickled across her tongue.

'That's enough,' Mum said furiously.

'I . . .' Lydia began.

'You didn't mean to hurt her, did you?' the reporter asked Lydia sympathetically.

Lydia shook her head. She hadn't hurt Frankie. It had been an accident. The reporter quickly scribbled in his notepad. He frowned up at the sky as drops of rain began to fall on his pad, smudging the ink.

Someone else was on the path now. Lydia couldn't see their face. The person – a woman – was too busy taking photo after photo. *Snap! Flash! Snap! Flash!*

79

'Lydia, will you be visiting Frances in hospital . . . ? Have her family told you to stay away? Lydia . . . ?'

Question after question. They didn't stop. Carl Williamson pushed himself forward. The only thing stopping him from pouncing was Lydia's mum. She moved to block the doorway, trying to stop both the reporter and the photographer.

'That's enough!' Lydia had never seen her mum so angry. 'Move your foot!'

The reporter's foot remained on the doormat, effectively stopping Mum from closing the door.

'Right! I warned you.'

Click! Flash! Snap! Flash!

'Oww!' The reporter yelped and jumped back as the heel of Lydia's mum's shoe found his instep. She slammed the door shut so hard that the glass in the door rattled violently.

'He's lucky your dad wasn't at home,' said Mum after a lot of muttering under her breath.

'Mum, will Lydia's picture be in the papers?' Danny's voice was scared.

'Of course not!' Mum snapped. 'As soon as Frankie comes round, she'll tell everyone it was an accident and that will be that.'

'What happens if she doesn't come round?' Lydia whispered.

Mum didn't reply. Lydia ran to the window in the front room. She watched the reporter and the photographer – a slight woman with short cropped hair – walk slowly away from the house. The photographer took a few more photos of the house before shaking her head and saying something inaudible to the reporter. Lydia continued to watch them as they got into their car and drove away.

Lydia went back out into the hall. 'Mum, I know you only tried half an hour ago but . . .'

'I was just about to,' Mum smiled. She went over to the phone and started dialling. 'Hello? . . . Yes, I'm phoning about a girl called Frances Weldon. She was knocked down and taken to your hospital? . . . Yes, that's right. I just wondered how she was doing?' There was a long pause. Lydia hardly dared to breathe. 'No, I'm not family,' Mum admitted reluctantly. 'But my daughter . . . Oh, I see. Well, could you just tell me if Frances has regained consciousness yet . . . ? Right . . . OK. Thank you. Bye.'

'Mum?' Lydia whispered.

'Frances is still unconscious,' Mum replied.

'Is she going to die?'

Lydia's heart lurched violently at Danny's question, leaving her with a dizzy, nauseous feeling. She didn't wait for Mum's answer, but turned away and walked back into the front room. She sat down and curled her legs under her.

'No, Danny, leave her be. Lydia wants to be alone for a while,' Mum said softly.

Danny ran upstairs to his bedroom, while Mum

disappeared into the kitchen to start a late lunch. Lydia heard pots and pans being banged and bashed and clattered and kitchen cupboard doors being slammed shut. Upstairs, Danny started playing his radio at a volume that soon had Mum hollering up the stairs for Danny to turn it DOWN!

Lydia closed her eyes. There was Frankie losing her balance, her arms spinning frantically. Then they spun more and more slowly until Frankie was moving in slow motion; *falling* in slow motion. And through it all was the high-pitched screech of brakes, a sound so unbearable that Lydia put her hands over her ears but still it wouldn't go away. Lydia opened her eyes and shook her head as if to shake the image right out of her mind. It didn't work.

The long empty minutes dragged by as Lydia sat statue still in her armchair, watching the empty road.

Please let Frankie be all right. Please let her wake up. Please . . .

The words played over in Lydia's head like a CD track on repeat.

Unexpectedly, the phone in the hall rang, making Lydia jump. Danny came charging down the stairs.

'I've got it, Danny.' Mum beat Danny to it. 'You can go and turn that radio down so I can hear myself think.'

Mumbling under his breath, Danny charged back up the stairs.

'Hello? . . . Hang on a minute. DANNY, TURN THE VOLUME DOWN OR I'LL TURN IT OFF!'

The noise from Danny's radio was instantly reduced to a distant hum.

'That's better!' Mum muttered. 'Hello? Sorry about that. Hello?'

Lydia didn't pay much attention to Mum's conversation until she heard Mum say in a shocked whisper, 'Who *is* this?'

Lydia went out into the hall.

'Who are you? You've no right to say such things. You're sick!' Mum was livid. She was clenching the phone's handset so tightly that Lydia wouldn't have been surprised if she'd snapped it in two. 'You're a sick scumbag who needs help. I suggest you phone your doctor but don't phone here again.'

Mum slammed the phone down so hard that the telephone table rocked for a good few seconds.

'Who was that, Mum?' Lydia asked.

'No-one,' Mum said, tight-lipped.

Danny started down the stairs.

'Danny, go back to your room – now,' Mum ordered.

For once, Danny didn't argue. Mum's tone made it clear that now wasn't a good time to whine at her. The phone rang again. Mum snatched it up.

'Hello?' Her voice was granite-hard. Mum listened for a few seconds, then slammed the phone down without saying a word. Time stood still as she and Lydia regarded each other. Lydia didn't know who'd phoned but she could guess what they'd said. It had to be really bad to make Mum see red like that.

A key turned in the front door. Dad stepped into the house. His expression was something to see. Lydia had never seen him so blazing angry.

'Have you seen the car?' he asked without preamble.

Without a word, Mum stepped out of the house after Dad. Lydia followed them, a few steps behind. She got to the gate and gasped, horrified. Thick white paint had been thrown all over the bodywork of Mum's and Dad's gleaming new midnight-blue car. It covered the bonnet, the windscreen, the roof; it was everywhere. Lydia watched as drops of white fell past the mudguards onto the road. The drops seemed to beat time – *drip, drip, drip* . . .

Lydia looked around. Net curtains fluttered back into place.

'Thank you all so much for making us feel so welcome,' Dad called out bitterly. 'Welcome to Tarwich!'

And Mum burst into tears.

'Come on, Roxanne. It's all right. Don't let them get to you. They're not worth it.' Dad led Mum back into the house, his arms around her as Mum leaned against his shoulder. Lydia stepped aside as Dad and Mum walked back into the house. It was as if she wasn't there – as if she didn't exist. Dad didn't even look at her. Lydia trailed behind them, lost in misery.

Look at all the chaos she was causing. All the unhappiness and destruction. Everyone would be better off without her. If she went away, everyone would be glad. No-one would even miss her.

What am I going to do?, Lydia wondered desperately. *What am I going to do?*

And as she watched Dad take Mum into the living-room, it came to her. The clearest, calmest thought she'd had in a long, long time.

Go, Lydia. Just leave. Get away.

Within moments, she had on her winter jacket and was out the door without saying a word to anyone. Raindrops began to spatter on her face, but Lydia didn't care. She needed to get away – more than ever. Within seconds the rain was pelting down.

Lydia walked along, not going anywhere in particular. The rain beat at her, forcing her to turn up her jacket collar and clutch it tightly around her neck. She passed a bus-stop, just as a bus drew up beside it. Lydia glanced up at it. After a quick look around she jumped onto it, flashing her bus pass.

'Where's this bus going?' Lydia asked.

The bus driver raised her eyes heavenwards. 'Tarwich Moors West. It says so on the front of the bus. Can't you read?'

Lydia walked to the first empty seat and sat down. She turned her head to stare out of the window. She was glad it was raining. She wanted it to rain. She wanted it to pour.

The clouds above were almost charcoal-grey now, yet bathed with a strange yellow light. Huge droplets slapped against the window. They danced into each other as they ran down the grimy windowpane. Lydia squeezed her eyelids tight shut, trying to stop her cheeks from getting any wetter. It didn't do much good.

Lydia had never felt so tired. So tired and alone and lonely. She opened her eyes and leaned her head against the cool windowpane. The bus meandered through the Tarwich streets on its way to the moors. It chugged to a halt by a bus-stop outside a baker's shop.

I hate you . . . Lydia directed the thought at the shop. And I hate that bus-stop and I hate this bus and I hate everything in Tarwich. And I'll get back at all of you, the whole town. All the people and everything in this rotten place – you just see if I don't.

The rain pelted down harder as if goading her on.

The bus continued on its journey until there were the moors, stretching out as far as the eye could see. The rain was teeming down now. Lydia rang the bell and sprang up. She moved to the exit.

'Are you sure it's here you want, love?' the bus driver asked with concern. 'There won't be another bus along for at least half an hour.'

'This is my stop,' Lydia replied.

The bus driver opened her mouth to argue only to snap it shut again. With a sigh, she stopped the bus and with a hiss the doors flew open. Lydia stepped down and watched the bus move off until it was out of sight. In seconds her whole face was wet from the relentless rain. Lydia sighed. Now that she was here, she wasn't quite sure what she wanted to do next. With another deep sigh, she decided to walk over the moors for a while. She wouldn't go too far by herself – she'd been warned about how easy it would be to get lost on the moors – but she wanted to get off the road. The thought of meeting anyone . . .

'Please, God, please let Frankie be all right,' Lydia begged.

It *had* been an accident. Lydia hadn't wanted anything to happen to Frankie. But now everyone thought she'd been responsible for Frankie getting knocked over. Gossip and innuendo travelled around the small town of Tarwich quicker than summer lightning. And when Frankie woke up she'd probably say the same thing as Anne. Lydia burned with hatred for everyone and everything around her. She gulped back a sob when she remembered all that paint on her Mum's and Dad's car . . . and the phone calls . . . and the net curtains fluttering . . .

Everyone in Tarwich was so nasty – cruel and nasty.

If only she could just stop the world for a moment, just long enough to catch her breath and think. If only . . . But what good did 'if only' do?

The ground beneath Lydia's feet grew softer and stickier as she left the road and started out over the vast moors. The rain lashed at her face and the wind howled like a banshee. Lydia was bent almost double as she struggled against the wind. And still she walked on, letting her feet choose her path as she tried to figure out what she should do next.

Please let Frankie be OK . . .

Please let her say it wasn't me . . .

Would that reporter really put pictures of her and her house in the *Tarwich Mercury*? Maybe Mum and Dad would lose their jobs because of her? Maybe Mr Simmers would believe that she really had wanted to hurt Frankie – or worse still, *kill* her . . . Maybe . . . Lydia bit down on her bottom lip – hard. She'd had enough of maybes and if onlys.

She rubbed a weary hand over the back of her neck. A sudden flash of lightning made her jump. It was almost immediately followed by a deafening boom of thunder. Lydia looked up at the sky. The charcoal clouds made the sky almost as dark as twilight. It couldn't be that late already. Surely she hadn't been walking for that long? Rain-water ran into her eyes and over her lips into her mouth.

Lydia straightened up to get her bearings. She gasped. The strange, swirling colours she'd seen in the car park were back . . . They filled the sky ahead, moving ever closer towards her. But directly above her the sky was still dark grey. The rain-water running into her eyes made everything around her swim and blur. Lydia blinked heavily and turned to try and spy the road. What was that in the distance? It had to be the bus-stop. She thought she saw it, way over to her left. She couldn't have walked so far away from it – could she? Lydia headed towards it, keeping her eyes on it. She didn't even want to look at those strange colours in the sky any more. Ahead, it was getting darker. With each step she sank up to her ankles in mud. The rain battered at her, making her face tingle, almost hurting her skin.

Then came a thudding sound, so faint at first that Lydia could hardly distinguish it from the rain. The sound came out of nowhere. Closer and closer it came. Closer and closer. The thudding changed to a pounding. Lydia looked in the direction of the noise. Through the dark sheet of rain she saw something making for her at great speed. Lydia opened her mouth to scream. The next moment a moor pony crashed into her as it galloped by in a panic. The force of the collision spun Lydia violently around and the ground came up rapidly to meet her. Lydia felt herself falling. She felt a sudden, sharp pain as her head hit the ground, but the falling didn't stop. Round and round. Lydia spun like an autumn leaf dancing with the wind. And then she was falling through all the colours in the sky. Lydia's last thought before darkness closed over her mind was that the strange, swirling storm had trapped her. Would it ever let her go?

Ten

A Change In The Weather

Sunlight warmed Lydia's face. Daylight, bright and welcome, seeped past her eyelids. Lydia thought about opening her eyes, then decided against it. If she didn't open her eyes then maybe the relentless pounding in her head would fade. She was wrapped in a cloak of silence and, in spite of her throbbing head, felt strangely relaxed, peaceful. It was an almost forgotten feeling. But then she remembered . . .

With a start, Lydia sat up. Her eyes flew open to their limits. Her right hand flew to her head as the pounding intensified. It all came flooding back. Thief . . . and the accident and running away . . . The storm . . . What had happened to the storm and the rain and the sky full of rainbow colours that had rushed towards her and swallowed her up?

There'd been a moor pony, galloping in a mad panic straight towards her. Lydia looked around, mystified. She must have fainted. No . . . she must have been knocked unconscious. But for how long? Long enough for the clouds to disappear and the sun to come out? Lydia put her hands down on the ground to steady herself, her head swimming and spinning again.

Something was wrong.

She filled her hands with earth and let it fall off her palms and trickle between her fingers. It was *dry*. The ground was dry. Lydia wiped her hands on her jacket. Her jacket was wet. It didn't make any sense. How could her jacket be soaking wet from the storm and yet the ground be bone dry? She looked around again. The moors stretched out all round her and the ground was not just dry, but cracked and parched. Lydia looked around for the bus-stop. *It wasn't there.*

She scrambled to her feet, her head turning this way and that. There was nothing – just space and silence. Something was wrong. Something was *different* – but Lydia had no idea what. She wasn't even sure why things felt different. Except for the ground being dry and the disappearance of the bus-stop, everything was the same as before, more or less. *More or less.*

Lydia slowly rubbed her nape. Why was her skin prickling? It was as if every hair on the back of her neck was standing to attention. Just at that moment, Lydia got the terrifying feeling that there was someone – *something* – behind her. Her head whipped around. Far off, above the horizon, the sky was ablaze with colour. Lydia stared, stunned, afraid. Flaming pink, orange and yellow swirls of colour whirled around and around. Lydia could see lightning crackling between the horizon and the sky, although she couldn't hear a thing. But the mad storm was still there.

What was it?

For a brief moment, she'd thought she'd only dreamt about being caught up in the strange storm. But there it was . . .

And one thing was certain – the storm was once again heading her way. The look of it, the *feel* of it, sent a chill stealing down her spine. Lydia had to get away. Fast.

She turned and started running in the opposite direction. She stopped abruptly. There, in the distance, a figure was running along. Lydia was too far away to see if it was a woman or a man, a girl or a boy, but someone was definitely there.

'HEY! HANG ON!' Lydia shouted. She ran to intercept the person. Halfway towards them, she shouted again.

'STOP! PLEASE STOP!'

Lydia kept running, perspiration trickling down her forehead. The person turned in Lydia's direction, then walked a few steps towards her. Lydia was now close enough to see that it was a girl of about her age, wearing a neck-to-ankle overall, dotted with different-coloured speckles and swirls. Lydia had never seen anything like it before. The material shimmered like glittery paper. Lydia looked around. Where had the girl come from? There was the road, but where was the bus-stop? And what had happened to the rain? Why was the ground dry? Questions buzzed around Lydia's aching head like angry flies.

'Who are you?' the girl called out suspiciously. 'I don't remember seeing you before.'

'I'm Lydia. When did the storm stop?' she asked, still running.

The girl frowned deeply but said nothing. Lydia was close enough now to see the girl's face. Her eyes flew wide open.

'Frankie? You're OK? Thank God, you're OK! What are you doing here?' Lydia rushed forwards. The girl took a hasty step back.

'My name's Fran, not Frankie,' said the girl. 'Who *are* you?'

Lydia blinked hard. Now that she'd had a longer look, she could see that it *wasn't* Frankie. This girl's hair was longer and a darker shade of brown and her eyes were dark brown, not green like Frankie's. But in everything else she looked exactly the same . . .

Lydia stared at the girl. 'Are you Frankie's sister?'

No, that didn't make sense. Two sisters would hardly have the same name.

'I don't have a sister. My name is Frances, but I hate Frances so everyone calls me Fran.'

Frankie's real name was Frances too . . .

Lydia's hand flew to her pounding head. She closed her eyes, swaying unsteadily.

'Are you all right?' Fran was immediately concerned.

'I . . . I don't know. I d-don't think so,' Lydia replied faintly.

Fran raced forward, only just managing to catch Lydia in time before she keeled over. Lydia breathed deeply, trying to fight off the feeling of nausea that was tumbling her stomach around like clothes in a washing-machine.

'You'd better come with me,' Fran said. 'We can't stand here chatting all day. We've only got ten minutes before curfew and I don't know about you, but I don't want to get caught by the Night Guards.'

'The Night Guards? Who are they?' Lydia asked.

'Huh? Don't they have Night Guards where you're from?'

'I'm from London. I mean . . . I was, until I moved up here,' Lydia said, confused.

'London! You escaped from London?'

'Pardon?'

'Never mind that now. You can tell me how you escaped later. Right now, we have to get home.' Fran helped Lydia to walk, still supporting her weight.

Lydia noticed the road in detail for the first time.

Before it had been smooth tarmac, but not now. Now it was rucked and the tarmac was broken. Broken blocks of concrete were scattered here, there and everywhere.

'What happened to the road?' Lydia pointed.

'What d'you mean?' Fran frowned.

'Did the storm really do this? Or has there been an earthquake, or something?' Lydia asked, confused.

'It's always been like this.' Fran looked as confused as Lydia felt.

Lydia watched Fran. If Fran was playing a trick on her, then it was a very good trick. Fran even managed to keep a straight face so that she didn't give the game away. And Lydia still couldn't get over just how much Fran looked like Frankie.

I must be dreaming, Lydia thought. I'm probably still lying on the moors and dreaming all this.

That had to be the explanation! So the best thing to do was to go along with the dream until she woke up. She just wished it made a bit more sense.

'I feel a bit better now,' she said. She straightened up and took some more deep breaths.

'Where d'you live?' asked Fran.

'Rosemary Street,' Lydia replied.

'Where?'

'Fourteen, Rosemary Street.'

'Never heard of it. Where's that?' Fran frowned.

Before Lydia could answer, an ear-piercing shriek filled the air. It was so loud that Lydia's hands immediately flew to her ears. Just as abruptly as the noise had started, it stopped. Lydia barely had time to open her mouth before the noise began again. Four more sharp blasts filled the air like the screech of a high-pitched, gigantic whistle. Her fingers in her ears, Lydia waited for yet another blast. None came.

'What on earth was that?' Lydia gingerly removed her fingers from her ears.

'We only have five minutes until curfew.' Fran looked around, worried.

'Curfew?'

'Yeah, at eight o'clock.'

'What?' Lydia looked around. When she'd left home it hadn't even been two o'clock yet. Eight in the evening and it was only just beginning to get dark. In November it got dark before five o'clock . . .

'We'll have to go for it now or we'll never get home in time. Are you up to running?'

'I think so. Where are we going?'

'My house. I don't know where Rosemary Street is and we don't have the time to go looking for it. Come on.'

Fran started racing along the road, jumping over the concrete blocks littering the road like a mountain goat over rocks. Lydia had no choice but to follow her.

This is the strangest dream I've ever had in my life, she thought to herself as she ran.

A couple of minutes passed before Lydia had to stop to unbutton her jacket. She was sweltering. She caught up with Fran and they carried on racing flat out without exchanging a word.

As they approached the town, Lydia was stunned by what she saw. That afternoon on the bus, she had passed shops and houses and neat gardens. They had all disappeared. In their place were several single-storey buildings surrounded by wire fences and barbed wire. The street was covered in mountains of rubbish and mounds of debris and rubble. There was an eerie silence all around and the very air smelt stale and unpleasant. Lydia took a number of short breaths so that she wouldn't have to breathe in too much of the foul smell surrounding her.

The ear-splitting siren sounded again, even louder than before. Except now the shriek was continuous.

'Jump down!' Fran shouted.

'What?' Lydia couldn't hear a word above the noise of the klaxon.

'Jump down!' Fran pointed to the embankment sloping away from the road. At Lydia's puzzled look, Fran grabbed her arm and pulled her off the road. They rolled down the embankment together. Lydia winced as her knee hit something sharp and hard. Fran placed her finger over her lips, then beckoned to Lydia to follow her. They crouched low and ran but the embankment soon petered away.

Then the siren stopped . . .

'We've got to get out of here. Curfew's started.' Fran ducked low and ran behind the nearest pile of junk and rubbish.

'What's that place?' Lydia pointed to the bungalows.

'The Night Guards' camp, of course,' Fran whispered. 'Surely you've seen one before?'

'Where did all this come from? I don't . . .'

'Shush! Keep your voice down,' Fran hissed. 'Follow me.'

Fran began to crawl along the filthy ground, edging towards the next mound of rubbish. With a frown of distaste, Lydia straightened up and started walking behind Fran.

'What're you doing?' Lydia asked.

'GET DOWN!'

Too late!

Without warning, a white laser blast like a rigid flash of lightning cut across Lydia, only just missing her. Lydia heard a low, distant boom and a second later her upper arm felt as if a fiery poker had been thrust into it. She shrieked with agony, clutching her left arm. The pain was intense, red-hot. A wet, sticky warmth ran down her arm and over the back of her hand down to her fingers. Lydia fell to her knees, the pain was so extreme.

Her arm felt like it was on fire. She stared down at the wide, blood-drenched tear in her left jacket sleeve and her jumper and shirt beneath. She was too stunned to even blink. Her whole body trembled with a coldness, more profound than any she'd ever experienced before.

Fran struggled to pull Lydia to her feet.

'*Come on.* Hurry.'

Lydia stared at Fran with unseeing eyes.

'*Please*,' Fran begged, yanking at Lydia's right arm.

Lydia struggled to get to her feet. If only it wasn't so cold . . . When did it get so cold?

'This way. Quick!'

Fran raced for the nearest half-demolished building, dragging Lydia along behind her. They zigzagged as they ran with laser bursts lighting up the twilight and low booms sounding around them. One laser blast missed Fran's head by mere millimetres.

Lydia wasn't cold any more. She was burning up. Her face was bathed in perspiration and she felt so sick. A sudden whirring noise behind them grew louder and louder. Terrified, Lydia looked over her shoulder as she ran. Bewildered seconds passed before Lydia realized exactly what was making the noise. It was a car – a car flying several metres above the ground and speeding towards them. A giant beam like a huge searchlight shone from the car's underside and danced along the ground after them. And Lydia could hear footsteps pounding behind her, getting closer and closer, but she couldn't *see* anyone. That almost made the footsteps worse than the car that was rapidly gaining on them. If only her arm would stop throbbing. If only her lungs would stop aching. If only she could stop for just a second . . .

'Come on!' Fran urged.

The pain in Lydia's arm grew worse with each step she took. She clutched her left arm and gulped for air as she ran. They ran through a wrecked house and out into what must have once been a back garden. Except now it was just a mound of earth and dirt and more rubbish. Darting between the obstacles, Fran pointed to what looked like a narrow storm drain, its entrance strewn with bricks and rubble.

'In here!' Fran ordered.

Lydia ducked down and scrambled after Fran into a dark tunnel that led steeply downhill. The tunnel was so low that the top of it pressed down relentlessly on her back. Lydia moved as fast as she could which wasn't fast at all because she was almost bent double.

'Get down,' Fran urged.

With a grimace, Lydia dropped down flat. Only just in time. Another laser beam flashed over their heads. Lydia wanted to freeze all this. She wanted a PAUSE button to press which would stop all this confusion and bring back the real world. She wanted something, *anything*, that would stop her arm from hurting so much.

'Come on.' Fran started crawling forward on her stomach, with Lydia close behind her. The front of Lydia's jacket immediately felt wet. They were crawling through about three centimetres of water – at least Lydia fervently hoped it was water!

'Turn right,' Fran commanded.

Lydia followed Fran to the right, then the left, then the left again as they snaked along. Lydia used her knees and only one hand to push herself forward, her other arm lying useless at her side. The small tunnel was now no more than fifty centimetres high. Lydia's arm throbbed painfully but it was just about bearable.

'We can stand up now,' Fran whispered after a long while.

Lydia looked around but everything was shrouded in pitch blackness. She couldn't even see Fran who was right in front of her.

'How can you tell?' Lydia asked.

'I know these tunnels like I know my own house,' Fran replied. 'Hang on a minute though.'

And then unexpectedly there was light. Fran sprang to her feet and moved her wrist around. The light was coming from the watch she wore. Lydia stood up slowly. They were now standing in what looked like a large, gloomy cave with more tunnels than Lydia could count leading off in all directions. Some of the tunnels were more than twice Lydia's height, some were so small that a mouse would have had trouble getting through them. A thirty-centimetre ledge circled the cavern but beyond that there was a drop into dark nothingness. Lydia moved forward and peered down warily. She couldn't see to the bottom of the pit. She straightened up and clutched her left arm tighter. Now that they'd stopped moving, her arm was beginning to hurt worse.

'This way.' Fran began to edge her way along the ledge. Lydia looked over the edge again. She didn't like what she saw – not one little bit. And she was tired and the whole left side of her shirt, as well as her jacket sleeve felt horribly cool and sticky.

'Can't we stop now?' Lydia asked.

'No way. It's not safe. They're still after us.'

'Who are they?'

'The Night Guards.'

'But why?' Lydia was totally confused. 'Why're they chasing us?'

Fran turned to face Lydia. 'Why d'you think?' she snapped.

Lydia didn't answer.

'To kill us, of course,' Fran said stonily.

Eleven

Hensonville

'In every town I know about, the Night Guards are ordered to shoot to kill after curfew. Don't you know that?'

Even in the dim torchlight, Lydia could see the suspicion on Fran's face.

'I thought you said you were from London?' Fran questioned.

'I am from London,' Lydia replied.

Silence.

'I don't feel well.' Lydia's mouth kept filling with saliva. She had to swallow over and over to stop herself from being violently sick.

'Who *are* you?' Fran asked.

Before Lydia could answer, a strange click-clicking sound filled the air.

'Oh no! They've sent the tracker mobiles after us. Move!' Fran continued shuffling round the ledge. Lydia looked back towards where the strange sound was coming from. Then she looked at Fran. She wanted to ask what a tracker mobile was but one look at Fran's frightened expression and Lydia decided that maybe it was better if she didn't ask. Not yet at any rate.

Lydia edged after Fran, leaning as far back into the wall as she possibly could. They passed a number of tunnel entrances at foot and waist level and still Fran continued making her way round the cavern. Then all at once Fran disappeared. The light from her watch vanished and Lydia was swallowed up by darkness.

'Fran! *Fran!*' Lydia whispered desperately.

Lydia peered through the darkness, her eyes huge, but she couldn't see a thing. And the clicking noise was getting louder and nearer. There was something in the regular, rhythmic click-click that sent a chill like an icy finger, stroking its way down Lydia's back.

'Lydia, in here.' A hand shot out from nowhere and Lydia was pulled backwards into a tunnel she hadn't even realized was there. Fran rolled a boulder that was balanced on castors and placed upon a track back across the entrance. She kicked against something on the ground. The castors and track sunk into the earth. The boulder rocked ominously for a moment, then was still. Only then did Fran switch off the light from her watch.

'Shush! Don't say a word,' Fran whispered.

Lydia bit her lip and closed her eyes and clutched her left arm tighter.

Wake up, Lydia! Wake up, now! she told

herself. She opened her eyes slowly. She was still in the tunnel. Fear bubbled and boiled inside her as the muffled clicking noise suddenly stopped on the other side of the boulder.

Fran's unexpected hand on her arm almost made her cry out. Icy perspiration trickled down Lydia's forehead into her eyes. Fran withdrew her hand immediately. Then, without a word, Fran took hold of Lydia's right hand and led her slowly down the inky-black tunnel. At least this one was almost as tall as Lydia so she didn't have to stoop too much. She opened her eyes wider, trying to see beyond the dark.

At last the queasy feeling in Lydia's stomach lessened. Neither of them spoke, but oddly enough the silence was almost comforting. They turned left, then right, before Lydia lost track of which way they were going. She wasn't sure what she was more afraid of – what lay behind her or what lay ahead. At least that sinister clicking had gone. Though they were travelling in the dark, Fran didn't pause or hesitate once. Several minutes passed until at last she stopped.

'There's a ladder here,' Fran whispered. 'I'll go up first then help you up.'

'Up where?'

'To my house,' Fran replied.

Lydia listened to Fran climbing the ladder. The torch in her wrist-watch was switched on again and shone on a keypad. Fran glanced down at Lydia's puzzled face.

'You have to input the correct code or the door won't open. It's the same for all the houses around here,' she explained, keying in an alphabetic code. 'Mind you, a coded keypad wouldn't stop the Night Guards if they ever found out what we're doing.'

There was a loud buzz and the door above Fran sprang open. Fran climbed up before she turned and reached down a hand towards Lydia.

'Come on. I'll help you up,' she said.

Lydia stepped onto the ladder. She used her feet and her one good hand to hoist herself upwards, until she reached the trapdoor. Fran took hold of her hand after that which made the going easier. She climbed through the trapdoor and Fran kicked it shut.

'Well, we got away with it.' Fran breathed a sigh of relief. 'This way. My dad will fix your arm.'

They walked across the basement filled with upturned, plastic crates, the strangest vacuum cleaner Lydia had ever seen – she only knew what it was because it said so on its side – and past other things she didn't recognize, towards a set of stairs. Lydia followed Fran up on to the ground floor. Fran shut the door carefully behind them. Lydia looked around. At last, here was something she could understand. A normal house with carpet and stairs and pale pink wallpaper and pictures hanging on the walls.

'Fran! Where on earth have you been? Who's this?'

Lydia backed hastily away from the man glaring down at her. He was a huge man, solid as an oak tree except for his stomach which had the beginnings of a distinct bulge. His short-cut, dark brown hair covered the sides of his head – on top he was as bald as an egg. But the way he regarded Lydia . . . He looked as if he was about to pick her up and swallow her down in one bite.

'Dad, this is Lydia,' Fran said quickly.

'Lydia what? I don't recognize her. Whose daughter is she?'

Silence.

'I don't know,' Fran admitted.

'You brought her back to our house using the underground tunnels and you don't even know her full name?' The veins in Fran's dad's temples bulged out ominously.

Lydia took another hasty step backwards.

'Her name is Lydia,' Fran began. 'And I thought . . .'

'No, you didn't think, Fran. That's your problem, you never think.' Fran's dad turned his attention to Lydia. 'Listen, you! I don't give a stuff what your name is. I want you out of my house – now.'

'But . . . but the curfew. The Night Guards . . .' Lydia began.

'Dad, you can't send her back out there. The

Night Guards will kill her for sure,' Fran argued.

'Fran, what's happened to your sense? This girl could be one of them. She could be a spy.'

'Me? A spy?' Lydia couldn't believe her ears.

'She's not, Dad. The Night Guards fired their EM rifles and laser guns at both of us. Lydia's injured. They wouldn't have done that if she was one of them,' said Fran.

'Grow up, girl,' Fran's dad growled. 'If she's one of them, then firing at her would make us think she's on our side, not theirs. It's a common tactic.'

'I'm not a spy. I swear I'm not,' Lydia protested weakly.

'Where d'you live?' Fran's dad asked.

'Rosemary Street. Number fourteen,' Lydia whispered.

'Liar!' Fran's dad bellowed at her. 'There's no Rosemary Street in Hensonville.'

'Where?' Lydia's lips began to quiver. Her head was aching, her arm was throbbing and the sick feeling in her stomach was back. 'I don't live in Hensonville. I don't even know where that is. I live at number fourteen, Rosemary Street, Tarwich.'

Tears began to trickle down Lydia's cheeks. 'And I want to go home,' she sniffed.

'Tarwich?' Fran's dad stared at Lydia. 'Tarwich . . . I haven't heard that name in a long, long time.'

'Dad, you know where it is?' Fran asked.

'Fran, sixteen or seventeen years ago *this* place used to be called Tarwich,' her dad replied.

'It was?' Fran stared at her dad. She turned to Lydia. 'Lydia, how did you know that?'

'Yeah! I'd like an answer to that question too,' Fran's dad said.

'I didn't . . .' Lydia whispered. Where was Tarwich? *This place was Tarwich.* Only now the name had changed to . . . to something else.

Henson-something . . . Her surname and something else.

When had the town's name changed? And why? Who were the Night Guards? Why had they tried to kill her? What had happened to the moor road? Where did the tunnels under the town come from? What was going on? Unanswered questions spun around in Lydia's mind.

'Answer the question. You're a spy, aren't you?' Fran's dad's face was only millimetres away from Lydia's.

Lydia stepped away rapidly until her back hit against a corner of the wall. Lydia put out her hand to steady herself. Out of the corner of her eyes Lydia saw the wallpaper around her slowly begin to change colour. She turned around and stared at it. The wallpaper had been a pale pink colour but now it was turning into a deep, sun-yellow.

'Look at that!' Fran's dad pointed to the wallpaper with disgust. 'She's afraid!'

'The wallpaper . . .' Lydia breathed.

'You're turning it yellow.' Fran frowned. 'It's mood wallpaper. You put your hands on it and it turns different colours depending on how you're feeling. Why're you afraid?'

'I . . . I . . .' Lydia couldn't get another word out. If only the hammering in her head would stop – just for a second.

Fran and her dad started asking more questions, both of them speaking at once. Lydia watched as their questions grew fainter and fainter until she could see that their lips were moving but could hear no sound. Fran turned to her dad and started shaking his arm. Lydia watched as Fran pointed at her while she spoke, but still Lydia couldn't hear what was being said. Both of their faces began to spin around her. Lydia's legs vanished from under her and with a groan she felt herself falling, falling, falling.

Lydia opened her eyes slowly.

'How're you feeling? You've been out for ages.' Fran was smiling down at her.

It took a few moments for Lydia to focus properly.

'You gave us quite a shock there. We didn't mean to scare you,' Fran said. 'We didn't realize you were so badly hurt. You've lost a lot of blood.'

Lydia turned her head. She was in a bedroom, smaller than her own at home. The walls were painted white with splotches of paint all the colours of the rainbow dotted here, there and everywhere. A huge screen, like an enormous TV screen, entirely filled one wall but it was switched off. Apart from the screen and the bed, there was not a lot else in the room.

'It was touch and go there for a while,' Fran carried on. 'Those EM rifles are deadly. You're lucky the bullet just sliced across your arm, otherwise it could have taken your whole arm off. Dad says you're lucky it wasn't more serious.'

'What's an EM rifle?' Lydia frowned.

'An electro-magnetic rifle.'

Lydia was still none the wiser. She looked around again.

'Is this your room?'

Fran nodded, then she smiled. Lydia stared at her.

'You really look like someone else I know,' Lydia couldn't help saying.

'Then I feel sorry for the other person. I hate the way I look,' Fran said with disgust.

Lydia and Fran exchanged a small smile.

'I'm sorry about what happened,' Fran said slowly. 'But Dad was right, I should have been more cautious. We have to be very careful about who we trust these days.'

Lydia didn't reply. What could she say?

'How's your arm?' Fran asked.

'Not too bad. It doesn't hurt as much now.'

'Dad had to staple it.'

'He had to do *what*?' Lydia stared.

'Calm down! Dad used to be a nurse. Your arm was badly cut so he had to staple it,' Fran replied.

'Staple it? With metal staples?'

'Of course not. He used medical staples.'

Lydia looked unconvinced.

'They're made of a special plastic,' Fran explained. 'As your arm heals, the staples will dissolve. I'm sorry but Dad didn't have a chance to close the wound in time. He says you're going to have a permanent scar there.'

Lydia sat up and gingerly felt her left arm. 'At least your dad has stopped it hurting.' She shrugged. That was all she cared about at the moment. 'Does he still think I'm a spy?'

'You were so badly hurt that he's not sure what to think any more,' Fran admitted.

Lydia still didn't understand what was going on. 'Is he always that suspicious of every person he doesn't know?' she asked.

'He has to be. We all do. It wouldn't be the first time that the Night Guards have tried to plant spies amongst us,' Fran said.

'Why?' Lydia asked.

Fran's eyes narrowed. Her expression turned ice-cold. 'Because we hate the Tyrant. We fight back against him in any way we can. And one day we'll win.'

'The Tyrant?'

'He owns this town. The Night Guards work

for him. He hates us,' Fran said bitterly.

'How can someone own a whole town?' Lydia frowned.

Slowly Fran shook her head. 'You don't know anything, do you? All the towns in this country are owned by someone. After Scotland and then Northern Ireland became independent, more and more regions in England and Wales decided to go the same way. When the central government in London collapsed, each region was supposed to vote in their own governors. But everyone knows all you need is enough money and then you can buy any town you want. And once you've bought a town or city, no-one interferes. Some regions do OK; some like us in Hensonville don't.'

'But why would anyone want to buy a whole town? I mean, what would you do with it once you had it?' Lydia asked.

'The Tyrant makes our lives a misery. He hates us. Every day he comes on the viewscreen and tells us how much he despises us and we're all forced to listen to him,' said Fran.

'That's the viewscreen?' Lydia pointed to the huge screen which covered one wall.

Fran nodded.

'Why does this Tyrant hate you all so much?' Lydia asked.

Fran shrugged. 'He just does. He arrived from London one day and took over this town. I think my mum discovered something about him just before she was killed by the Night Guards, but she never got the chance to tell me what it was.'

'Does your dad know?'

Fran shook her head, adding, 'At least that's what he says.'

'I . . . I'm sorry about your mum.' Lydia wasn't sure what to say.

Fran shrugged and looked down at the floor. 'It was a long time ago. I can hardly remember her.'

'I wouldn't have thought that made it any better,' said Lydia.

'It doesn't,' Fran admitted.

'This Tyrant sounds like a nasty piece of work.' Lydia shook her head.

'He is. Lots of people have been taken to his mansion by the Night Guards. Not one of them has ever been seen again,' said Fran.

Lydia shivered. 'I don't know where I am or what's going on, but I wish I was at home!'

'Dad's in a meeting with the others of the Resistance. He's going to ask them about you. Maybe we can help you get home,' Fran said. 'Dad reckons you came from another town but you're suffering from shock caused by your arm injury. He reckons that's what has made you so confused.'

Lydia had heard that shock could do that to you, but she didn't think that was her problem. The first thing she had to do was sort out what on earth was going on.

'This, er . . . Resistance you were talking about? Is that like in the Second World War when some people secretly fought against the Nazis?' asked Lydia.

Fran shook her head. 'I don't think I should say any more about that. I've said too much already. Dad would bust a blood-vessel if he knew.'

'I won't tell him if you don't.'

After a moment's silence, Lydia and Fran giggled conspiratorially. Fran glanced down at her watch.

'Dad's meeting should be well under way by now. I'll see you later,' she said.

'Where're you going?' asked Lydia. She didn't fancy being by herself.

Fran's voice lowered. 'I'm going to listen in on Dad's meeting.'

'Can I join you?' Lydia asked.

'I don't think . . .'

'Please, Fran. I need to find out what's going on. I don't know where I am or what I'm doing here and nothing makes any sense.'

Deep frown lines creased the skin around Fran's mouth.

'You can trust me – I promise,' said Lydia. 'I'm not a spy. I'm not about to betray you to this tyrant person. Besides, I wouldn't know him if I tripped over him. *Please?*'

Fran sighed heavily. 'OK then, but for heaven's

sake, don't make any noise. I'm not supposed to be listening to them either.'

Fran gave Lydia a clean shirt to wear. It felt very strange – almost papery – but once Lydia put it on it was very warm. She tucked it into her jeans and together the two girls crept out of the room and down the stairs. Fran put her finger over her lips as they tiptoed to the basement door. Slowly, oh so slowly, Fran turned the door handle. She beckoned Lydia over and they both listened.

'. . . and you're wrong,' one man's voice argued vehemently. 'If we get rid of him, how do you know he won't be replaced by someone even worse?'

'There is no-one worse,' a woman's voice said bitterly.

Lydia strained closer.

'Getting rid of him sends out a clear message that tyrants and dictators won't be tolerated in this town,' said another man's voice.

At least five different voices started arguing amongst themselves. Suddenly they all stopped, like a radio being switched off. Fran's hand was already on the door handle, ready to shut the door in a hurry, when a new woman's voice said quietly, 'The Night Guards killed my husband and my son. I have more reason to hate them and that murdering Tyrant than any of you. But none of you are thinking logically. I say we should . . .'

Lydia drew away, horrified. She couldn't listen to any more. What was going on in this strange place? *Where was she?* She pulled Fran away from the door.

'Fran,' she whispered. 'Why doesn't your dad and all the other grown-ups just call the police or get the government to do something?'

Fran shook her head. 'Lydia, the Night Guards *are* the police. And the Tyrant *is* the government – at least as far as this town is concerned.'

Lydia stared at her. Something very bizarre had happened from the time when Lydia was knocked out on the moors, but she had no idea what. It was like waking up in the middle of Wonderland. No matter which way Lydia turned, nothing made sense.

Fran beckoned Lydia back to the door.

'If only he had some family,' said a second man's voice. 'Then we could kidnap his wife or children and have something to bargain with.'

'I heard they did that with the ruler of Leeds!' said a woman Lydia hadn't yet heard speak.

'He's too smart to have a family and for exactly that reason,' said the first man bitterly. 'Henson would never allow himself to do the things normal people do – like have a family.'

Lydia felt as if she'd just been kicked in the stomach. She froze.

'What's the matter?' Fran asked, concerned.

'W-What's the tyrant's name?' Lydia could barely get the words out. 'His full name?'

'Everyone knows that,' Fran replied. 'It's Daniel Henson.'

Twelve

Answers

'Daniel Henson . . .' Lydia breathed. It wasn't, it *couldn't* be her brother. Lydia closed her eyes tight and fought against the panic that rose within her like a tidal wave.

'Lydia, are you all right?'

'My brother's name is Daniel Henson,' Lydia said weakly.

'Your brother?' Fran was appalled.

'Yeah . . . he's . . . he's ten.' Lydia's voice trembled.

There was a deathly silence. Then Fran started to giggle. 'For a moment there I thought . . . Well, never mind what I thought! Imagine thinking the Tyrant is your brother! The Tyrant is pushing fifty and you're what? Twelve?'

Lydia nodded.

'The same age as me,' Fran said, but Lydia hardly heard her.

A possible explanation for what was happening crept into her mind, but she shook her head. It was too bizarre, too ridiculous to be true. It couldn't be. But the thought refused to leave her head. Lydia had a new question now. Not where was she, but *when* . . . ?

'What's he like – Daniel Henson?' Lydia forced herself to ask.

Fran's smile vanished. 'He's old and ugly and mean. He's been the ruler of this town since before I was born.'

Lydia's fingernails dug into her palms.

'When was that?' she asked.

'Don't you know your own birthdate? 2020. Why?'

Lydia stared at Fran until her eyelids started to hurt and her eyes began to ache.

'What year is this?' Lydia whispered.

'2032. You should know that – you're the same age as me. Can't you count?' Fran's eyes narrowed. 'Look Lydia, you're worrying me. Maybe I should call my dad . . .'

'No! Don't!' Lydia looked around quickly. 'I . . . I need to sit down.'

Lydia walked over to the bottom step and sat down before Fran could stop her. Closing her eyes she pinched her left forearm. She clicked her heels together again and again. Then she opened her eyes slowly. She wasn't lying in her own bed. She wasn't even back in Tarwich. The wallpaper surrounding her was still a brilliant, burning yellow. Was this all real? Was Lydia really in the future? It was impossible, ludicrous – and yet, here she was . . . Fran stood in front of Lydia, a bewildered look on her face.

'Fran, could you touch that wallpaper please?' Lydia asked.

Fran walked over to the wall and did as Lydia asked. Jets of maroon and burgundy spread outwards from her hands.

'What do those colours mean?' asked Lydia.

'Confusion!' Fran smiled drily. 'And you're the one confusing me!'

Lydia looked around. When she'd first arrived at the house she'd only really noticed the things that were the same as in her time. Now she could see the things that were different.

The strange-shaped light bulbs dotted around the ceiling but no light-switches anywhere that Lydia could see. The viewscreen, the tracker mobiles, the peculiar wallpaper, even the strange papery shirt that Lydia was wearing. Lydia took the bottom of her shirt in both hands and tried to tear it. It was like trying to tear a pair of thick tights.

The year 2032 AD . . .

Lydia still couldn't believe it. And yet here she was. It had to be true. What other explanation was there?

I can't be dreaming. Surely I'd have woken up by now if I was dreaming, Lydia thought.

'How d'you switch your lights on?' she asked,

looking up at the light bulbs decorating the ceiling.

'Hall lights on!' Fran said, puzzled.

Immediately every hall light came on.

'And to turn them off?' Lydia asked.

'Hall lights off!' frowned Fran. 'Is this some kind of joke?'

Lydia shook her head. A joke? If only it was. Then Lydia remembered something her mum always said whenever she and Danny hadn't tidied up their rooms.

'Who cleans the house?' Lydia asked. 'Is that you and your dad?'

Fran's frown deepened. 'Our house robot of course. It's only a model GH-1042-A so it's really slow but it gets the job done – eventually.'

Mum was always saying, 'If you two are waiting for someone to clean your rooms for you, you'll have to wait until some time in the twenty-first century when housework robots are available. Until then, get to it!'

So Mum was right. Housework robots were coming!

'The Tyrant won't allow anyone he doesn't absolutely trust to have any robot that's more advanced than the model GH-1042-A,' Fran added bitterly. 'He's probably afraid we'll re-program them or something and send the robots after him.'

Lydia walked over to the heavy curtain which hung from ceiling to floor before the front door.

She pulled it aside. The front door wasn't made of wood. It was made of steel.

'How d'you get in and out?' Lydia asked Fran.

'There's a keypad outside and a control switch inside.' Fran frowned.

'So you don't need a key?'

'A key for what?'

'It doesn't matter.' Lydia let the curtain fall over the door again. She looked up. Sprinklers had been placed at regular intervals along the ceiling. All of the downstairs wallpaper was covered in a mass of pink and burgundy swirls now.

'What're you doing?' Fran asked curiously.

'I'm not asleep. I'm not dreaming all this, am I?' Lydia said slowly. 'This isn't 1995?'

'This is the year 2032. I just told you,' Fran said.

All the pieces of the puzzle were beginning to fit together. Lydia swallowed hard. Somehow the storm on the moors must have pitched her forward in time – thirty-seven years into the future . . . It was impossible – and yet here she was in the year 2032. And the searing ache of her arm was too painful to be anything but real.

And Daniel Henson . . . Was he really her brother or was it just a coincidence? Daniel Henson was a common enough name. It *couldn't* be her brother. He'd never do all the bad things that everyone was talking about. He would never do anything to be so *hated*. Never. But what if it *was* her brother . . . ? Then something else occurred to Lydia.

'Fran, what was your mum's maiden name? Her full name?'

'Frances Weldon. I was named after her. I wish Mum and Dad had picked something else. I really hate the name Frances,' she grumbled.

Frankie . . .

So Fran was related to Frankie after all. Frankie was Fran's mother. That meant that Frankie was all right. She'd survived the accident and woken up. She'd even grown up and had a daughter. Lydia's smile faded. Fran said that her mum had died when she was a lot younger – killed by the Night Guards. Lydia wanted to cry because she wasn't sure how she felt. Relief that Frankie had survived her accident in 1995, but then what? To be killed so violently, so horribly . . .

Maybe, in 1995, she and Frankie had made up? Maybe the truth had come out about the sports cup? Maybe – hopefully – they'd become better friends than ever before?

'I really *am* in the future,' Lydia realized.

'What did you say?' Fran asked.

Lydia stood up slowly. She had a problem. She needed help, desperately. But could she trust Fran? Would Fran turn her back on her just as Frankie had done? Even now a flare of the old burning bitterness swept through Lydia's body. Just as quickly, it died. She had a more urgent problem now. How was she going to get back to her own time of 1995? Beside that, every other problem was minuscule. With a sigh, Lydia realized that she didn't have any choice. She needed Fran's help.

'Fran, I need to talk to you.'

Just at that moment, Fran's dad emerged from the basement.

'Fran, what's she doing down here?' He frowned.

'Lydia was thirsty, Dad. We just came downstairs for a drink,' Fran replied quickly.

'Hhmm! Well, get your drink and go back upstairs,' said Fran's dad.

'I've already had it. We were just on our way upstairs again,' Lydia said.

'Is your meeting over then?' Fran asked her father.

He nodded before turning to Lydia.

'Come here,' he beckoned.

After a brief nod from Fran, Lydia did as she was told. With reluctant steps she made her way over to Fran's dad.

'Let's see your arm.'

Fran pushed up the left sleeve of her shirt. Fran's dad carefully removed the bandage. Then Lydia saw her wound for the first time. It was S-shaped and looked like a snake weaving its way up her arm. Placed at regular intervals along the wound were the grey, plastic staples which Fran had told her about. Lydia lifted her arm and bent her head for a closer look, but she didn't get it! Fran's dad reapplied the bandage, thwarting her attempt.

'It's just as well you were with Fran when the Night Guards shot you,' Fran's dad growled. 'Any longer and your arm could have been seriously infected.'

'I thought you thought I was a spy,' Lydia reminded him.

'I said *you* were lucky, I didn't say *we* were.' Fran's dad sniffed. 'Now keep that sterile dressing on for at least two days.'

'Yes, Mr Weldon,' Lydia said.

'The name is Mr Lucas. Shaun Lucas. Not Weldon,' said Fran's dad. 'That was my wife's name.'

'Sorry,' Lydia murmured.

Lucas . . . ? Shaun Lucas . . . ? Lydia stared at the man before her.

'Frankie married *you*?' She grinned with delight. Just wait till she told Frankie that she was going to marry Shaun Lucas!

It was only when she saw the deepening frown on Fran's dad's face that Lydia realized what she had said.

'Er . . . I'm sorry . . .' Lydia began. 'I didn't mean . . .'

'Never mind!' Fran's dad shook his head. 'No doubt the pain in your arm is affecting your mind.'

He straightened and bent her arm, gently turning it first this way, then that.

Shaun Lucas . . . He was the first one who'd called her a thief . . .

'Your arm will be fine,' said Fran's dad.

'Thank you.' Lydia pulled her arm out of his grasp.

Mr Lucas frowned suddenly, leaning closer to Lydia.

'You look kind of familiar. Have I seen you before?'

'No, you haven't,' Lydia denied, flustered. 'I'm new here. I . . .'

Fran tugged at Lydia's sleeve. 'You said you wanted to talk to me,' she interrupted.

Lydia nodded and quickly ran upstairs ahead of Fran. She was aware of Fran's dad standing at the bottom of the steps, his eyes boring into her back. They entered Fran's bedroom and Lydia closed the door carefully behind her.

'Fran, the weirdest thing of my entire life has just happened to me . . .' At Fran's puzzled look, Lydia broke off.

'What's the matter?' Fran asked.

'Fran . . .' Lydia began slowly. 'I need to see Daniel Henson.'

'Are you nuts? What on earth do you want to see him for?' Fran asked, appalled.

'I can't explain but I have to see him. Can you get me into his mansion?'

'Don't you understand? If you go in there, you'll never come out again.'

'I'll risk it.'

'Why?'

'I can't tell you. Not yet at any rate.'

Fran scrutinized Lydia. 'You're serious, aren't you?'

Lydia nodded.

'I'm not going to help you unless you tell me why,' Fran said stubbornly.

Anxiously, Lydia chewed her bottom lip. This was it. What should she do?

'Fran, I'm twelve years old but . . . but I was born in 1983,' Lydia said slowly.

Silence.

'I don't understand,' Fran said at last.

Carefully picking her way through the words, Lydia explained what had happened from the time she got on the bus which took her to the moors. She couldn't bring herself to talk about the sports cup being found in her locker and her classmates calling her a thief. That wound was still too raw, too painful to expose.

'. . . so I woke up on the moors and the ground was bone dry. The rest you know,' Lydia finished.

'You're from the *past*?' said Fran, slowly.

'Look, if someone told me this story I wouldn't know what to think either!' Lydia said. 'I'm finding it hard to believe as well and it has actually happened to me.'

Fran grinned suddenly. 'This is a wind-up – right? Where are you really from?'

'1995. You've got to believe me.'

Fran's scepticism was obvious.

'What can I do to prove it?' Lydia pleaded. 'I *am* from 1995.'

'Turn around. Let me see your ID implant,' Fran ordered.

'My what?'

'Your identity implant,' Fran said impatiently.

Lydia turned around. 'What's one of those?' she frowned.

Fran carefully examined Lydia's nape, from the bottom of her hair-line to where the back of her neck joined her shoulders.

'You don't have one . . .' Fran whispered, astounded.

Lydia turned around. 'What are these . . . implants?'

'The moment anyone's born, they get an ID implant put into the back of their neck. They're tiny, computer chips that look a bit like old-fashioned buttons. The implants tell who you are, who your parents are, date of birth and other stuff that they call – classified,' Fran finished with a scathing snort.

'But why? What're they for?'

'They're meant to be the way of knowing who everyone is, especially those who move around a lot. The leaders of every town have implant readers, so you can't lie about your identity. And then of course they can call up your file and get your full background and history.'

'We don't have those in 1995.' Lydia shuddered with relief. What a horrific idea. Having a computer chip installed in your head from the moment you're born . . .

'They started using implants in this country in 2008,' Fran said slowly. She turned Lydia around and examined her nape again. 'Everyone who's twenty-four or under definitely has one, and most people over that age too, unless they've gone underground. Of course you could have had yours surgically removed . . . but then there'd be a scar. You don't even have a scar . . .'

'That's because I'm not from your time. D'you believe me now?'

The two girls spent countless moments just watching each other.

'You're telling the truth, aren't you?' Fran's voice was filled with wonder. 'H-How did it happen? How exactly did you get here?'

'I don't know. I'm not sure.' Lydia sighed. 'I'm here with you, but I don't belong here. I belong in 1995 and I've got to get back.'

'How're you going to do that?'

'I don't know. That's why I have to see Daniel Henson.' Lydia lowered her voice.

'But why? He's . . .'

Fran stared at Lydia, her eyes getting wider and

wider as at last she realized what was on Lydia's mind.

'I think Daniel Henson *is* my brother. And if he is, he's the only one who can help me,' Lydia said.

'How?'

'He's the only one around here who knows what happened to me. If he's my brother he can tell me what happened . . . happens to me. He'll know how I got back to my own time,' explained Lydia.

'*If* you got . . . got back,' Fran said.

'If,' Lydia agreed. 'Now do you understand why I must see him?'

Thirteen

Mike

Fran jumped up off the bed and paced up and down the room. Lydia watched her, her heart in her mouth. What would Fran do? Would she tell her father . . .

'Maybe there's a way for you to find out what you need without having to speak to the Tyr . . . er . . . to Daniel Henson,' Fran said.

'How?'

'My dad might know. He might be able to help.'

'No! I don't want anyone to know that I might be related to Daniel Henson. Not until I know for sure,' Lydia said firmly. 'If . . . if he is my brother then I want to find out what's going on. I want to ask him why he's doing all these terrible things.'

'And you think he'll tell you?' Fran raised her eyebrows.

'I'm his sister.'

'He's ancient and you're twelve! If he is your brother, why should he tell you anything?'

'Because I'm still his sister,' Lydia replied, adding with a smile. 'His older sister!'

Fran smiled reluctantly.

'Fran, I can help you, all of you. I'm sure I can,' Lydia persisted.

'OK, but let's talk to my dad first. He'll . . .'

'NO!' Lydia interrupted. 'I don't want him to know who I am. Promise me you won't tell him.'

'I promise. I'll be careful what I say. Trust me,' Fran said.

They regarded each other for a few moments. Then Lydia nodded.

'OK,' she said at last, knowing that she didn't have much choice. Lydia knew that she wasn't being fair to Fran. Just because Frankie had let her down, that didn't mean that Fran was going to do the same. But Lydia felt like deep inside she was holding her breath, just waiting for Fran to do the same thing as her mother.

Frankie's death . . . Was Daniel Henson responsible for that, too? Lydia sighed, a peculiar, hollow ache inside her. She hoped that she and Frankie had become good friends again. She hoped that very much.

Lydia followed Fran downstairs and into what Lydia assumed was the living-room. A huge, black table dominated one end of the room. At the other end, closer to the door, were a couple of armchairs and some other kinds of chairs that Lydia had never seen before. They looked like hammocks with backs, perched between cylindrical, metal pedestals. Another huge viewscreen completely covered the wall opposite the door.

'Dad?' Fran called out. 'Dad?'

'What's the matter, Fran?' Fran's dad appeared behind them, making both Lydia and Fran jump.

'Dad, I need to ask you something,' said Fran.

'Let's sit down then.' Fran's dad followed them into the room.

Lydia tried out one of the hammock chairs. To her surprise it was much more comfortable than it looked. Fran sat next to her dad.

'Dad, what did the Tyrant do before he bought Hensonville?' Fran asked.

Fran's dad glanced quickly from Lydia to his daughter.

'No-one knows,' he answered. 'He came from London but that's about all anyone has been able to find out about him.'

'Where's the rest of his family?' Lydia asked.

She held her breath as she waited for the answer. Fran's dad shrugged.

'I don't know about his parents. He had a sister once but no-one knows what happened to her. Why d'you want to know?'

'I just wondered,' Lydia whispered.

A dead end. Fran's dad didn't know anything about her.

Fran stood up. Lydia followed her lead. But before they'd taken a step, the viewscreen crackled. Without warning, a man's face and shoulders appeared on the viewscreen. The face by itself was at least two metres high. The man's lips were turned up in what was supposed to be a smile but the man's dark eyes were ice-cold. Lydia felt an electric chill shoot down her back. She didn't recognize the man's face at all, but looking into his eyes was like looking into a mirror at her own . . .

'Good evening, citizens of Hensonville!' the man said. His voice dripped with sarcasm like blood from a vampire's fangs.

Lydia turned to look at Fran and her father. They both glared at the screen. And the looks on their faces made Lydia's heart jump in her chest. The air between both of them and the screen almost crackled with their hatred. Lydia's blood ran cold as she watched. She felt sudden fear. Would Fran keep her promise?

'It has come to my attention that some of you are still roaming the streets after curfew,' the man continued with a snake-like smile. 'Once again it is my duty to remind you that if you are caught outside after curfew, you cannot hold me or my Night Guards responsible for the consequences.'

'Let's get out of here before I throw up!' Fran's dad said with disgust.

Fran turned to Lydia, her eyes narrowed. She tugged at her dad's arm.

'Dad . . .'

In that instant every sound and every sight in the world melted away. There was just Lydia and Fran – and what Fran would say next.

'Dad, can Lydia and I go to Mike's?' Fran asked at last.

'At this time of night?'

'Please, Dad.'

'Why?'

'Lydia and I need to talk to him. It's urgent. *Please*.'

Fran's dad looked from Lydia to Fran, then smiled. 'Oh all right then. But use the tunnels and be careful.'

'Come on, Lydia.' Fran smiled.

Lydia slowly smiled back. She followed Fran out into the hall and down into the basement.

'I thought . . . I thought you were going to tell your dad about me,' Lydia said at last.

'I wouldn't do that,' said Fran simply.

They entered the tunnels and travelled in silence for several minutes with only the yellow-white beam from Fran's wrist-watch to light the way. Lydia tried to memorize the route they were taking but in less than two minutes she was totally lost. It was dark and smelly in the tunnels and Lydia wished that the torch in Fran's watch was a lot stronger. Ahead and behind them the torchlight was quickly swallowed up by shadows and darkness. And it was so quiet.

'Who're we going to see?' Lydia whispered.

'A friend of mine – Mike Joyce. I don't know the way to the Henson mansion. Not via the underground tunnels at any rate,' said Fran. 'But Mike does.'

'Will he help me?'

'I don't know. Mike's OK. I don't like his mum much though. My mum always said she couldn't be trusted.'

They carried on walking, lapsing into silence. Minutes passed.

'We're here,' Fran whispered at last.

She shone her torch on a ladder that led up to another trapdoor with a keypad beside it. Fran climbed up first. She keyed in several letters of the alphabet before pressing the <ENTER> key. A door swung open.

Once up the ladder, they walked through the basement which was almost identical to the one in Fran's house. It was filled with junk and discarded furniture so they had to pick their way through it carefully.

At the top of the basement stairs, Fran opened the door which led into the hall. Lydia wrinkled up her nose at the dusty, musty smell. And there was an unpleasant pervasive aroma behind that – kind of like sour milk or food that was just beginning to go off.

They stepped out into the hall which was even more full of clutter than the basement. Broken bits of furniture and machinery were strewn throughout the hall and even old bits of crockery were lying about. In one corner of the hall was something covered with blue-green mould. Lydia decided she'd keep her distance from *that*! It looked like something out of a horror movie. If she got too close, it wouldn't have surprised her if the mould leapt up and bit her ankle! Mike's house was a total contrast to Fran's house.

'They leave the house like this because every time they clear up, the Night Guards arrive and smash the place to pieces again,' Fran explained.

'Will they mind us just coming into their house like this?' Lydia frowned.

'Mike and I are like brother and sister. In case of emergencies, I have his code and he has mine.'

'Oh, I see.'

A tall boy with light-brown hair and dark-brown eyes emerged from the living-room. Lydia reckoned he must be about fifteen or sixteen.

'Oh Fran, it's you,' he smiled. Then his smile abruptly vanished. 'Who's that?' The boy pointed to Lydia but didn't look at her. His eyes never left Fran's face.

'Hiya, Mike. This is Lydia. She's a . . .'

'Did you come via the tunnels?' asked Mike.

'Yeah, but . . .'

'Fran, you shouldn't have brought a stranger through the tunnels,' Mike said coldly. 'Did you show her my access code?'

'No, I promise,' Fran answered quickly. 'She didn't see it, did you Lydia?'

Lydia shook her head. Mike turned to look at Lydia for the first time. His eyes narrowed. Lydia looked at Fran, uncertainly. What was wrong with this boy? What was wrong with everyone she'd met so far in Hensonville? Were they this unfriendly with everyone? Was this what the Tyrant had done to them?

Mike scrutinized Lydia without blinking until it was all Lydia could do to stop herself from squirming on the spot.

'Mike, Lydia is my friend,' Fran said, pointedly.

Mike relaxed visibly. 'I'm sorry to be so unwelcoming, but I'm sure you can appreciate why we have to be so careful.'

Lydia nodded but said nothing. She wasn't sure about Mike.

'Now that both of you are here, what d'you want?' Mike asked brusquely.

Lydia and Fran exchanged a look.

'He's a real charmer, isn't he?' Fran chuckled.

'Mike! Who're you talking to?' A woman's voice called from up the stairs.

'Fran and a friend of hers,' Mike called back.

'That's Mike's mum – Mrs Joyce,' Fran whispered to Lydia.

A tall, blond woman began to walk down the stairs, her attention focused on tightening her belt around her overall. Before Lydia could do more than glance at her there came a sudden urgent banging on the front door which echoed like thunder all around them.

'THIS IS THE NIGHT GUARDS. OPEN UP IN THERE!'

'Fran, Lydia – get lost! Now!' Mike didn't mince his words.

Without another word, Fran pulled Lydia into the basement.

'OK! OK! I'm coming,' Lydia heard Mrs Joyce call out.

Leaving the door slightly ajar, Fran ran for the trapdoor to the tunnels. But there was no time. Desperately looking around, she ducked down behind a huge box, pulling Lydia after her. Lydia knelt down, careful to make sure that no part of her body could be seen past the box.

'Squat, don't kneel. It's faster to jump up and run that way,' Fran whispered.

Lydia did as directed, just as heavy footsteps ran into the hall.

'Mrs Joyce, you're to come with us,' a woman's voice said.

'Not again,' Mrs Joyce said wearily.

'Now!' the woman commanded.

'Mike, stay here and take care of things,' Mrs Joyce said.

Even though her voice was firm, Lydia could hear a slight quiver behind her words.

'Mum, I . . .'

'Keep back!'

Mike cried out in sudden agony. Lydia gasped at the sound.

'Mike!' Mrs Joyce's voice was frantic.

'I'm OK, Mum.' Mike's voice gurgled strangely.

'Come on,' the woman's voice ordered.

'Take your hands off me. I can walk,' Mrs Joyce said bitterly.

'Mum, will you . . . ?'

'Mike, I'll be OK. Take care,' Mrs Joyce said softly.

The heavy footsteps retreated and the front door closed. Lydia sprang up. Fran pulled her back down again. Only just in time too. The basement door opened and a strong flashlight shone around the room. Lydia didn't dare move. She closed her eyes and held her breath. Soft footsteps entered the basement. Lydia bit down hard on her lip to stop herself from crying out. She felt that close to panicking.

'Nothing upstairs,' said a man's voice from outside the basement.

'It's clear in here too,' said a second man, waving his torch around one last time.

Then the footsteps retreated together. Lydia heard the front door open, then close again.

Moments passed. Lydia let out her breath through her mouth in a slow, barely audible hiss.

'You can come out now,' Mike said from the door.

Fran and Lydia stood up and ran out of the basement up to the hall. Mike stood against the wall, his left hand leaning against it for support. His right hand held a filthy cloth to his bloody nose.

'Are you OK?' Fran asked.

'I'll live,' Mike said bitterly.

'What was that all about?' Lydia whispered.

'The Tyrant, of course. It's his regular dose of harassment. He hates my mum more than anyone else in this whole town.'

'Why?'

'I don't know – and Mum won't tell me.' Mike leaned his head back against the wall. 'But every week we go through this. The Tyrant treats my mum like a cat playing with a mouse.'

Lydia swallowed hard.

Don't let it be Daniel. Let there be some mistake. Please don't let it be my brother.

Brilliant, gleaming white spread out from Mike's left hand across the wallpaper like ripples on a pond. The white was so bright it hurt Lydia's eyes.

'Fran, what does white mean?' Lydia asked, pointing to the wallpaper.

'Anger,' said Fran.

'And hate . . .' Mike added softly.

Fourteen

Captured!

'Mike, we need your help. Lydia, you explain,' said Fran.

Mike straightened up and gave his nose one last wipe before throwing the filthy cloth into an already crowded corner of the hall.

Lydia took a deep breath, forcing herself to look away from the wallpaper. 'I need to get into Daniel Henson's mansion.'

The silence in the hall could have been cut with a knife. Mike dabbed at his nose with the back of his hand. He sniffed tentatively, then wiped his nose on his sleeve.

'You're new to Hensonville, aren't you?' he said at last.

Lydia nodded.

'I thought I hadn't seen you before,' said Mike.

'Will you help me?' Lydia asked.

'Why?'

'I think . . . I think I might know him. If I could just talk to him, I might be able to stop all this,' Lydia replied.

'No. I mean, why should I help you? What's in it for me?'

'Mike!' Fran said, shocked.

The question threw Lydia for a few moments. 'I . . . er . . . I don't have any money.'

'I'm not interested in money,' said Mike, coldly. 'What good will that do me or anyone else in this town?'

'What d'you want then?' Lydia asked.

'You know Daniel Henson?' Mike said.

'I . . . I think so. I'll need to speak to him to find out,' said Lydia.

'And what makes you think that his Night Guards aren't going to shoot you on sight?' asked Mike.

'I'm willing to risk it. I *need* to see him.'

'I'll help you get into his mansion but only on one condition,' Mike said at last.

'What's that?' Lydia prompted.

'If you get to see the Tyrant, I want you to promise that you'll make sure I'm with you,' said Mike.

'I promise,' Lydia said at last. She didn't have much choice.

Mike smiled silkily. 'Let's go,' he said.

Five minutes later, Lydia, Mike and Fran were back in the underground tunnels which twisted and turned under the whole of Hensonville. They walked in eerie, echoey silence for a while. The light from Fran's watch cast a dull yellow light which in turn cast deeper shadows all around them.

'Where did these tunnels come from?' Lydia whispered, more to hear the sound of her own voice than for any other reason.

'In the twentieth century they used to be part of the town's sewage system,' Fran explained, 'but they've been modified and extended since then. The Tyrant and his guards have no idea how much.'

Lydia wrinkled up her nose. The sewage system! What was she stepping in?!

'The tunnels have been extended to run into the woods behind the Henson mansion,' Mike continued. 'The woods are part of the Henson estate so we should be able to get into the house without the Night Guards realizing that we're even there. There's a whole network of tunnels beneath the woods of the Tyrant's estate, but I'll take us out of the tunnel closest to his mansion.'

'How come you know the way to the Henson mansion and Fran doesn't?' Lydia asked.

'My mum is one of the leaders of the Resistance,' Mike said proudly.

'So she tells you everything?' Lydia asked, surprised.

'She has to – in case something happens to her,' said Mike. 'We both know that the day may come when the Night Guards take her away and she doesn't come back – when the Tyrant decides that just tormenting her isn't as much fun as it used to be.'

They travelled on in silence until Lydia couldn't stand it any more.

'Mike, er . . . how old are you?'

'Sixteen.'

Sixteen . . . Just a few years older than her and yet he seemed so much older. Lydia hated the year 2032. It was dangerous and threatening and frightening. All she wanted to do was go home. The Collivale sports cup and being called a thief now seemed so trivial, so small by comparison to what was going on in this time. Lydia would gladly have traded one for the other.

'Look, I . . . I don't want to get you two into trouble. And I don't want either of you to get hurt,' Lydia said unhappily. 'Maybe it would be better if you just gave me directions and I went on by myself.'

'You'd never find your way to the Henson mansion by yourself,' said Mike. 'Besides, if you can really get the Tyrant to see you in person then I want to be there.'

Something ice-cold, ice-hard, in Mike's voice made Lydia turn and look at him closely, but his face was an unreadable mask.

'How long has the tunnel into Daniel Henson's house been there?' Lydia asked.

'It was finished a few days ago,' Mike said. 'One way or another, the Tyrant's time is up.'

'What does that mean?' asked Lydia.

'Just what you think it means,' Mike smiled. 'Soon the Resistance is going to strike out against him and he won't stand a chance.'

Lydia turned her head to see that Fran was watching her carefully.

'The Resistance are going to use the tunnels to get to him,' Lydia realized.

'Why else would we have built them?' Mike argued.

'What are you going to do with . . . with Daniel Henson once you have him?' Lydia asked.

'What d'you think?' said Mike bitterly.

And now, more than ever, Lydia knew she had to see Daniel Henson. His life and her future depended on it.

'Fran, take Lydia's hand and I'll take yours. You'll have to turn off your watch-light,' said Mike.

'How will we see where we're going?' asked Fran.

'I know the way by heart. Only a few of us know the way to the mansion and that's the way I intend to keep it,' said Mike.

Fran switched off her watch-light and they moved slowly forwards and downwards. To Lydia, it was like swimming through an ocean of black ink. She couldn't tell where the walls ended or where the ceiling started. She gripped Fran's hand tighter and wished she was in the middle of the three of them rather than at the end. Seconds turned into minutes which seemed to turn into hours. Lydia lost all track of time. No-one spoke. Lydia's breathing grew heavier as fear gripped her lungs and refused to let go.

What was she going to do? How was she going to get home? What if Daniel Henson *wasn't* her brother . . . ?

No, he had to be her brother. She had seen his face and recognized his eyes. They were Danny's eyes. Danny, who was ten years old the last time she saw him and now was what? Forty-six? No, forty-seven.

And then there was the question that Lydia wanted answered more than any other. What had happened to *her*? Where was the Lydia Henson of the future?

The path turned steeply upwards. Lydia's legs began to ache and she was soon out of breath.

'We're here,' Mike whispered. 'Once we get out into the woods, no-one's to say a word until we get into the mansion. We haven't fully established what kind of security the Tyrant uses in the woods so we'll have to be extra careful. Fran, the pattern to get to the tunnel underneath the old junior school is 4574R-F. You'll know your way home from there.'

'I'm not leaving the two of you.' Fran shook her head.

'You must. It'll be dangerous enough for Lydia and me. With you along we stand more chance of being caught,' Mike argued.

'Mike, I'm not going back,' Fran fumed.

'Fran, please. You know I'm right.'

Silence. Then Fran sighed deeply. 'Very well then,' she said reluctantly.

'What's the pattern to get to the old school?' Mike asked.

'4574R-F,' Fran repeated impatiently. 'I'm not stupid, you know.'

'Excuse me while I run after my head!' said Mike.

'I didn't mean to bite your head off but stop treating me like a brainless nerk-chip!' Fran grumbled.

'Can we get going now please?' Lydia interrupted. Now that they were so close she didn't want to waste any more time listening to Mike and Fran argue.

Fran let go of Lydia's hand and edged her way around her to start back.

'Lydia, stay exactly where you are until I open up the exit,' said Mike.

Lydia stood still, listening to Fran's footsteps receding behind her. Mike scraped what sounded like two pieces of stone together. Then all at once moonlight streamed into the tunnel. Lydia turned away, blinking rapidly. After the darkness of the tunnel, the moonlight was as bright as summer sunshine.

Mike beckoned with his hand. Lydia began to climb the dirt steps which were fortified with stone blocks. She stepped out into the night and looked up. Beyond the rustling leaves, she could see the moon and the stars. They were so beautiful. Here was a link to 1995. Even if the whole world had changed since 1995, at least the moon and the stars looked exactly the same.

Mike pushed a small boulder over the tunnel exit and covered it with branches and bracken. Without a word, Lydia helped him. She could see his face clearly in the moonlight. In spite of all his confident talk, Lydia could see that he was on the scared side of anxious. She nudged his arm to get his attention, then smiled at him. Mike smiled back. They both straightened up. Mike looked around.

He pointed to his right and they started walking in that direction. Barely had they taken two steps when huge searchlights like giant wolves' eyes appeared all around them. Lydia's head jerked this way and that as each light hit her with the force of a punch.

'Stand where you are!' said a voice from beyond the spotlights. Lydia shaded her eyes with her hand and tried to see who had spoken but the lights were blinding her.

Lydia looked around. They were surrounded.

'Lydia, run!' Mike shouted.

Mike grabbed her arm and pulled her after him. Out of the corner of her eye, Lydia saw a gun being pointed at them: not the person holding it – just the gun in front of the searchlights.

'Mike, no!' Lydia pushed Mike to the ground and turned. Immediately her lungs felt as if they were on fire. Lydia gritted her teeth. Her hands, clenched in fists, flew to her chest. In the moment before the darkness took her, she realized that she'd been shot . . .

Fifteen

The Meeting

Lydia woke up but didn't open her eyes. She didn't want to move any part of her body because it would only make the pain in her chest worse. She could hardly breathe. It felt as if a sumo wrestler was sitting on her. And her arm was throbbing badly. Lydia forced her eyes open and sat up slowly. Her breathing became easier but her head felt as if it'd just tripled in weight. Lydia looked around. Mike was lying on the floor across the room.

'Mike! Are you OK?' Lydia stood up. Pain lanced through her arm, making her gasp. She clutched her left arm and stumbled across the room towards him.

'Mike? Mike?' Lydia squatted down.

Mike opened his eyes, then sat up so quickly that Lydia had to jump back. He leapt to his feet.

'Where are we?' he asked, looking around.

'I don't know.' Lydia looked around as well. She was in a room unlike any she'd seen so far in this time. It had wood panelling on the walls instead of wallpaper and the furniture looked antique. A huge, ornate mirror dominated one wall of the room. Even the door was the old-fashioned kind made of wood instead of the sliding kind made of metal.

'We're in *his* mansion . . .' Mike whispered.

He ran to the door and tried to open it. It was locked. Lydia ran over to the curtains. Maybe they could escape by breaking the windows . . . Steel bars protected the glass, both inside and outside the window-frame. So much for that idea.

'What're we going to do?' Lydia asked.

'We have to get out of here. I've got to let the Resistance know that the Tyrant knows about our tunnel into his estate,' said Mike desperately.

'How did he find out?' asked Lydia.

'There's no way he could have found out . . . unless there's a traitor in the Resistance,' Mike said slowly.

'But if he knows about the tunnel, why didn't he just close it down?' Lydia asked.

Mike laughed grimly. 'Because he's clever. Because he's waiting for the Resistance to launch their attack and then he'll pick them off one by one, just as he did to us.'

Lydia's arm dropped to her side. She was in Daniel Henson's house – where she had wanted to be – but suddenly the prospect of meeting him filled her with fear which burnt like acid.

Lydia rubbed her moist palms into her crumpled jeans.

'I'm scared,' she admitted.

'Listen. The first chance one of us gets we've got to make a break for it and warn the others,' said Mike. 'Head for the woods.'

Lydia nodded. She understood perfectly.

Just at that moment, the door opened. Two Night Guards marched in. Lydia stepped back quickly. It was the first time she'd seen them close up. They were dressed in grey all-in-one suits and wore grey helmets like motorcycle helmets with visors so dark that Lydia couldn't see their faces.

'You!' one Night Guard said pointing to Lydia. 'Come with us.'

Lydia took another quick step backwards. She looked around quickly. There had to be somewhere to run, somewhere to hide . . . Her shoulders slumped. There was nowhere. The Guard didn't ask a second time. He stepped over to Lydia and seized her by her left arm. Lydia howled in agony but he didn't let her go. If anything, his grip tightened. Lydia's arm was on fire again, worse than before. She tried to pull away but it was impossible.

'Let her go!' Mike tried to help her but the second Night Guard stood between him and Lydia. Without saying another word, the first Guard marched Lydia out of the room. Turning left he strode down the corridor, past closed wooden doors on either side, towards the huge double doors at the far end of the corridor. He opened one door and thrust Lydia into the room. Lydia stumbled and fell. The door shut behind her with a resounding thud.

Lydia filled her mouth with saliva and told herself over and over again, 'Your left arm doesn't hurt! It doesn't hurt!' Her mum had told her once that this was a good way to stop aches and pains. You had to fill your mouth with saliva and tell yourself that a specific pain in a specific place wasn't there and didn't hurt. Her mum had called it 'mind over matter'. Strangely enough, after a few deep breaths, the pain in her arm did lessen slightly. Lydia stood up, still telling herself that her arm didn't hurt. She swallowed hard and looked around. The room was dark but not frightening. The only light came from a huge fire at the other end of the room. To her left was a window, partially covered with thick, heavy curtains which hung down to the wooden, parquet floor. Books and more books filled the shelves which reached from floor to ceiling on every wall.

'Come over here.'

The command made Lydia jump. She'd thought she was alone. She turned but couldn't see anyone. A high-backed chair was positioned in front of the fire. Slowly the chair swivelled around.

'Come over here.' An oldish man with greying

hair and a white-speckled moustache beckoned her over.

Slowly, Lydia did as she was told. The man turned his chair back to the fire as Lydia approached so that she had to walk around him. The moment Lydia was close enough, the man placed his hand under her chin and tilted her head towards the firelight. He tilted it upwards, then leaned it away from him.

'Lydia . . .' he whispered softly.

Lydia pulled her head away and stared at the man. His voice was deep and, even sitting down, he was taller than Lydia. He was wearing a dark jumper and what looked like corduroy jeans. This man was solid with a broad chest and a hard face.

But there was no doubt about it. Lydia recognized his eyes at once. The same eyes that had stared at her from the viewscreen in Fran's house. The same eyes as hers. She wanted to throw her arms around him and hug him. He was someone she recognized. He was her *brother*. But the words of every person she'd met since her accident on the moors kept darting around her mind.

The Tyrant . . . He despises us . . . He controls the Night Guards . . . Murderer . . . Tyrant . . .

Lydia didn't know what to do or say, so she said and did nothing.

Long moments of intense silence passed, broken only by the crackling and spitting of the log fire.

'Pull up a chair while I check on your friend,' the man said at last. He held up a remote control and pointed it at the wall above the fireplace. A small viewscreen suddenly flickered into life.

Lydia saw Mike pulling at the window-bars of the room she'd just been in.

'I've got to . . . get out . . . of here,' Mike puffed as he pulled and pulled.

Lydia turned to the man. He smiled with amusement and pressed another button on his remote control. Mike's image vanished.

Lydia walked over to the nearest chair by the fireplace and pushed it back towards Daniel. She sat down, never taking her eyes off this man who had to be her brother. What could she say? Where to begin?

'Are you Daniel Henson?' she asked.

'Of course,' the man replied. 'And what's your name?'

'Lydia. Lydia Henson,' Lydia replied.

'Ahhh!' said Daniel.

Why did Lydia get the feeling that he had been expecting that answer?

'How old are you?' Daniel asked.

'Twelve. How old are you?'

'Forty-seven.'

The memory of Daniel at ten years old popped into Lydia's head. She could see him sitting at the dinner table, grinning fiendishly as he ate with his mouth wide open. The image faded to be replaced by the man in front of her.

It was impossible to believe and yet here she was, sitting next to her grown-up brother.

'Daniel . . .' Lydia said slowly. 'You're my brother, Daniel.'

'Who sent you? The Resistance?' Daniel's smile was encouraging.

Lydia frowned at him. 'No-one sent me.'

Daniel studied her face closely.

'Who operated on your face to make you look like my sister?'

Lydia was shocked. 'No-one.'

'They did a very good job, whoever it was,' said Daniel. 'That's why I had you brought in here. You look exactly like my sister when she was your age.'

'I am your sister, Danny. And I need your help to get back to 1995.' Lydia pulled her chair closer to her brother.

'I'm still trying to figure out exactly what they thought they'd achieve by changing your face to look like Lydia's,' Daniel mused. 'Did they really think I'd believe that you were my sister? The Resistance must be getting desperate.'

'Danny, I *am* your sister. I promise. I went to the moors. It was raining and I was hit by a pony and the storm caught me and whirled me around.' Even to Lydia's ears, it sounded like she was rambling. 'Then I woke up to all this. You've got to believe me. It's the truth.'

'Prove it.' Daniel smiled.

Lydia didn't like his smile. Not one little bit. It was the smile of someone who was saying one thing and thinking something very different.

'How?' Lydia asked nervously.

'What was my nickname for you when we were kids?' Daniel asked.

'You didn't have a nickname for me.' Lydia frowned.

Daniel raised his eyebrows.

'Unless you mean that you used to call me Lyddy, but that's not really a nickname.'

Very slowly, Daniel started to clap.

'I see you've done your homework.' He smiled.

'What happened to you? Why are you like this? You're my brother, but not the one I remember.' Lydia shook her head.

'And what brother do you remember?' Daniel scorned.

'The Danny I knew was the only one to stand up for me when the school sports cup was found in my locker and everyone thought I was a thief,' Lydia replied. 'He was special. He wouldn't have grown up to be you!'

Daniel's oily smile had vanished now. Instead a deep frown turned down the corners of his mouth and his eyes were narrowed as he studied Lydia. Lydia couldn't stand it any longer. She leapt out of her chair.

'Why are you like this?' Lydia shouted at him. 'Why are you so horrible?'

'If you really were my sister you'd know why – and you'd thank me,' Daniel said coldly.

'I don't understand,' Lydia said. 'I don't understand anything in this place. I want to go home. Tell me how to get home. You're my brother, you should know.'

'Why?'

'Because you grew up with me,' Lydia said bewildered. 'I don't think I live here in Tarwich, I mean Hensonville, with you any more because no-one knows about me. Fran's dad said that no-one knows what happened to me. So tell me. Where am I? What happened to me? And how did I get home to 1995? You must know.'

'I've had enough of this act. Who are you?' Daniel's expression gave Lydia frostbite. She took a hasty step back, banging into her chair.

'I *am* your sister. Why won't you believe me? What happened to me?'

'You really want to know what happened to you?' Daniel asked, his voice so quiet that Lydia had to strain to hear him.

Her blood ran icy-cold in her body. Something was wrong, very wrong. She could see that from the look on Daniel's face.

'Follow me – Lydia Henson!' Daniel stood up, abruptly.

Without another word he strode across the

room and keyed in a password on the console beside the patio windows. The windows slid apart silently. Daniel strode out into the moonlit night. Lydia had to trot to keep up with him, he was walking so fast. She looked up at him. He was so much taller than her. He was her brother – something deep within her told her that – but he'd changed so much.

Daniel opened a gate and walked into a secluded part of the garden surrounded by a tall hedge. A large, light-coloured marble tower dominated the view ahead of them. It sat on a plinth, surrounded by lights which shone up at it. Lydia's steps faltered. There was something about that tower. Something which made her want to stay put and not get any closer to it. Even with the lights around its base, it still looked overpowering and for-bidding – like a malevolent giant just waiting to snatch her up.

Lydia looked up at Daniel, her heart sledge-hammering in her chest.

'It's a monument. A memorial. Go and look at it,' Daniel said silkily.

'I . . . I don't want to . . .'

'Go and read it,' Daniel ordered. 'You're not my sister and this monument proves you're a liar. Go on! Look!'

Trembling, Lydia turned and moved slowly towards the structure. She bent down close to read the words engraved deeply into the light-coloured marble, illuminated by the surrounding flood-lights.

'Lydia Angela Henson. Beloved daughter of Ben and Roxanne Henson. Beloved sister of Daniel. Lest we forget . . .' Lydia's voice trailed off into a shocked silence.

In that moment, the whole world froze.

'My sister is dead. She was killed by the people in this town,' Daniel said quietly. 'So why don't you tell me again how you're my sister?'

Sixteen

It's A Lie

Lydia stared up at Daniel. Even her arms wrapped tightly around her couldn't keep out the winter iciness that crept slowly down her entire body. Every part of her went numb.

She was dead.

She had died . . .

Here she was, watching, listening as her brother told her that she was dead. Lydia couldn't breathe, but it didn't seem to matter. It was as if every part of her, even the need for breath had been frozen.

She was dead.

'NO!' Lydia's scream was ripped from deep inside her. 'I'm here. I'm not dead. I don't believe it. I *won't* believe it.'

And all at once, every part of her burst into painful life. She gasped for breath to fill her air-starved lungs, her arm throbbed, her head was pounding – she was alive!

'I'm sorry to spoil your little game but con-gratulations on a fine performance.' Daniel smiled. 'It's not your fault that the people who put you up to this didn't do all their homework properly.'

'It's a lie. I can't be dead,' Lydia said, appalled. 'I *am* your sister. My name is Lydia Angela Henson and I'm twelve and this is . . . this is just a nightmare.'

Daniel's eyes narrowed. 'The art of playing a good game,' he said softly, 'is knowing when the game is over.'

'My name is Lyd . . .'

'Enough!' Daniel shouted at her. 'My sister was killed in a car crash five days before her thirteenth birthday. My parents were driving us to my aunt's house in London when it happened. I was there. So why keep on with this farce?'

Five days before her thirteenth birthday. Lydia's birthday was the eighteenth of December. Lydia swallowed hard. Back in 1995 it was only mid-November. Back in her own time she had just over three weeks before she was going to die . . .

Daniel folded his arms across his chest.

'What's your real name?' he asked.

Lydia didn't answer. She couldn't. All she could think about was how she only had three weeks in her own time before she was going to die in a car crash . . . That thought burnt through her, hurting more than the bullet that had sliced into her arm. Then she remembered something strange that Daniel had said.

'If I'm supposed to . . . d-die in a car crash, how come you said I was killed by the people of this town?' Lydia whispered.

'The people in this town forced us out. If it hadn't been for the way they treated all of us and especially Lydia, my mum and dad would never have wanted to escape to London for the Christmas holidays. The people in this town killed my sister just as surely as the lorry that ploughed into us on the motorway did,' Daniel said, stonily.

Lydia shook her head. 'But that's not fair . . .'

'Fair! Don't talk to me about fair. I swore after my sister died that I'd make them all pay and I'm keeping my promise. What happened in the past is nothing compared to what I intend to do to the people in this town in the future,' Daniel said bitterly. 'All I need to know is who the leaders of the Resistance are. I'll get that information from you and your friend, Mike. Then I'll crush them and their rebellion. And I'll enjoy doing it.'

Lydia stared at him, stricken. All this hatred, all this chaos, was because of *her*. The people in Tarwich had made her so miserable and she had thought she hated them so much, but looking at Daniel made all of Lydia's remaining hatred flicker and die for ever.

If that's what hatred did for you then she wanted no part of it. Everyone in Tarwich – or Hensonville as it was now known – was so unhappy and, for all his talk, Daniel was no happier. He was a bully and a tyrant. And worse still he was doing it for *her*. But Lydia didn't want this. Maybe once, but not now.

Lydia desperately tried to think of something to say that would convince her brother to stop, but before she could say a word, pain flared through her arm, up past her shoulder and down to her fingertips. She winced and laid her right hand over her wound. She could feel her shirt sticking to her skin. Her wound was bleeding again. When that Night Guard had grabbed her arm, he must have damaged some of the staples. Lydia pushed up her sleeve and looked. She was right. Blood was seeping down her arm.

Lydia looked up at Daniel. He was watching her suspiciously.

'What's wrong with your arm?' he asked, his eyes narrowing as he glimpsed the wound.

Before Lydia could reply, an insistent bleeping noise interrupted her. Daniel dug into his trouser pocket and took out what looked like a small, thin calculator. He pressed a button.

'Bring her to me,' a woman's voice ordered.

'Why?' Daniel asked the device in his hand.

Lydia took a step closer and craned her neck to see who Daniel was talking to but all she could see was a small viewscreen, the size of a pocket TV. She couldn't see who was on it. Daniel frowned at her and turned his back on her to continue his conversation.

Lydia took a quick look around. Now was her chance. She had to get back to the others to warn them that Daniel knew about their tunnel. She had to stop them from using it.

Lydia took off towards the woods in the opposite direction to Daniel, her heart racing faster than her legs.

'Hold your fire! Don't shoot! Get her!'

Lydia looked around, not slowing her pace for a second. Night Guards were racing after her from all sides. Lydia wondered frantically why Daniel had stopped his guards from shooting at her again. Was he beginning to believe that she really was his sister? Should she have stayed and tried to convince him that she was telling the truth? By running, would he think that he was right to doubt her?

Lydia reached the woods and ducking down low, she darted around tall trees which loomed over her like giants and low bushes which whipped at her legs. She couldn't stop. She couldn't let the guards catch her. Not until she had warned Fran and Mike's mum and the others in the Resistance.

Suddenly, Lydia couldn't see a thing. The moon disappeared behind a cloud and the stars were just tiny pinpricks of light above her.

Lydia stopped running immediately. She didn't want to run into a tree – or worse still a Night Guard! But what should she do?

Up ahead, through the trees she could see a faint pink shimmer, lightening the sky towards the horizon. She rubbed the back of her neck where it had begun to prickle.

Dawn must be coming up, Lydia thought. She hadn't realized that she'd been unconscious for so long after she'd been shot.

'Get those lights on. NOW!'

Lydia heard Daniel's angry voice in the distance. Almost instantly searchlights lit up the night. Lydia didn't hesitate. She raced towards the pale pink shimmering light. It didn't matter that with each step towards it her skin prickled more. Somehow she knew she had to get there.

'Lydia, quick! Down here!'

Lydia looked around. She could hear Fran's voice but she couldn't see her anywhere.

'Down here!'

A flash of light emerged from the gnarled surface roots of an old oak tree up ahead. Lydia raced for the tree. She threw herself down on the ground and crawled frantically into the small hole beneath the trunk. Even now she could hear the heavy, running footsteps of the Night Guards just behind her. Lydia tumbled past Fran down a couple of dirt steps. The burgeoning dawn light in the tunnel disappeared as Fran immediately blocked the entrance.

Shakily, Lydia stood up.

'Am I glad to see you!' Lydia breathed a sigh

of relief. 'I thought you'd left. Mike told you to get going.'

'Just as well I didn't get very far, isn't it?'

'Daniel and his Guards know about the tunnel.'

'Yes, I know. I heard them firing at you and Mike,' Fran said. 'We've got to get out of here.'

'We've got to get a message to the . . .'

'Shush!' Fran shook her head quickly and pointed above them.

Lydia got the message. The Night Guards were too close to risk talking. For all Lydia knew, they could be standing just by the oak tree, still looking for her. Fran took the lead and once again, Lydia found herself trekking through the tunnels beneath Hensonville.

'D'you remember Mike's instructions?' Lydia whispered.

'I think so. I hope so.' Fran's voice sounded worried.

'What d'you mean . . . ? Never mind.' Lydia decided not to ask.

Getting back to her own time was becoming more remote by the second.

Seventeen

Mrs Joyce

With each step, Lydia had to rub her neck harder and harder. Only now it wasn't just her neck that was prickling. It was as if each drop of blood in her body had turned into a tiny red-hot needle that was trying to pierce its way through her skin. She gritted her teeth and scratched the back of her legs and the front of her arms. It didn't help.

'Where are we?' Lydia risked speaking after at least thirty minutes of silence.

'Under the moors,' Fran whispered. 'It should be safe to come out here.'

'Why the moors?' Lydia asked. 'Why can't we just go back to your house?'

'The Tyrant knows that Mike and I are friends, so he'll send his Night Guards straight there, looking for you – and me,' Fran replied. 'And if we're found in anyone else's house it will be instant termination – for both of us and for the family that hides us.'

'I don't believe it . . .'

'It's happened before,' Fran insisted.

What could Lydia say? There was nothing to say.

'We'll have to lie low for a while,' Fran continued.

'On the moors?' Hiding on such a wide open space seemed like suicide.

'It's the best place – believe me.' Fran smiled.

'I suppose you know what you're doing,' Lydia said doubtfully.

They turned left and began to walk up a dirt slope. Fran pushed at some bracken and moss above her head at the top of the slope. Lydia closed her eyes and clenched her fists.

My skin isn't on fire . . . my skin isn't on fire . . . she told herself. It didn't work.

'Come on, Lydia,' Fran beckoned.

Lydia crawled out of the tunnel after Fran. She looked around. They were totally alone.

Then she saw it.

Rolling towards them from the horizon was a massive swirl of burning pink and flame-yellow and fiery-red – the same as before, when Lydia had run away from home to walk on the moors. It wasn't just some clouds that were heading their way. It was as if the whole sky was rushing towards them. Lydia stared up at the racing colours and her stomach dipped and dived within her. It was still the most frightening and yet the most beautiful thing Lydia had ever seen. Why did she feel so drawn to it and yet so repelled by it at the same time?

'What *is* that?' Lydia pointed.

'I don't know. I've never seen anything like it before.' Fran shook her head.

With great difficulty, Lydia forced herself to look away.

'What do we do now, Fran?'

Fran didn't hear her. She was still staring at the swirling sky colours.

'Fran?' Lydia shook Fran's arm. 'What do we do now?'

It took a few moments for Fran to come out of her reverie.

'Sorry,' she breathed. 'I'd better phone Dad and tell him where I am.'

Fran took out what looked like a credit card with numbers on it and started tapping the keys. Lydia moved closer to see what she was doing.

'What's that?'

'A viewphone,' said Fran.

'Why didn't you use it when we were in the tunnels? Wouldn't that have been safer?' Lydia asked.

'Viewphones don't work down in the tunnels.' Fran frowned. 'You really don't know anything, do you?'

'I'm from 1995 – remember,' said Lydia.

And Lydia remembered that it was the year she was supposed to die . . . She'd never see 1996 . . .

'So is Daniel Henson your brother?' Fran asked carefully.

Lydia nodded.

'Did he believe you?'

'No. According to Daniel, I died . . . his sister died in 1995,' Lydia said miserably. 'I tried to tell him about my accident on the moors but he wouldn't listen. He thinks I'm part of the Resistance and you've operated on my face to make me look like his dead sister.'

'You died in 1995?' Fran said, horrified. 'Oh Lydia . . . I don't know what to say.'

'Well, it hasn't happened yet. Meanwhile, I've got to make Daniel stop what he's doing. He hates this whole town and everyone in it because of me,' said Lydia. 'Because of *me*.'

'I don't understand.'

Lydia chewed nervously on her bottom lip.

'I . . . I didn't tell you the whole story before,' Lydia admitted. 'The reason I was on the moors in the first place was because . . . because I ran away from home.'

'Why?'

Lydia looked towards the swirling colours which were getting ever closer. She had to fight hard against the urge to run towards them. They were almost like invisible hands, pulling at her. She looked away.

'Everyone at my school thinks I'm a thief. The whole town thinks I'm a thief, but I'm not.

The Collivale School sports cup went missing and it was found in my locker,' Lydia said quietly. 'Everyone turned against me – even my best friend, Frankie. I got surrounded in the playground and called a thief. They wouldn't stop picking on me. Then Frankie had her accident and I got blamed for that too.'

'The Collivale sports cup . . .' Fran stared at Lydia.

'Yeah! Isn't that stupid?' Lydia smiled bitterly. 'It seems so far away, so *tiny*. All this started because of a school sports cup.'

Lydia closed her eyes and tilted her head back until she could trust herself to speak again. 'Frankie slipped on some ice. It was an accident but . . . but I can't help wondering . . . If I'd just been a bit faster, maybe I could have caught her and stopped her from falling. Or maybe if I hadn't slapped her hand away from me in the first place then she wouldn't have fallen . . .'

'Oh my God! That was *you*?' Fran stared at Lydia, profoundly shocked. 'Lydia, Mum didn't blame you at all. She always said it was her own fault. She slipped and you tried to grab her but you couldn't – that's what she told everyone.'

Lydia shrugged and looked away. 'Frankie was too late. I ran away because a reporter came to our house. And we started getting phone calls and Mum and Dad got paint thrown over their car.' Lydia shivered at the memory. 'Daniel told me that Mum and Dad were driving us to my aunt's house in London to get away from all the unpleasantness. That's when the motorway accident happened . . . happens. That's when I'm killed.'

'Lydia, I think . . .' Fran chewed on her bottom lip nervously. 'Hang on a second.'

Fran moved a few steps away from Lydia, then keyed some numbers into her viewphone. Within moments Mrs Joyce's face appeared, covering the whole device.

'Mrs Joyce, you're back! I was worried that the Night Guards might have decided to keep you for longer than one night,' said Fran.

'They've never got anything out of me and they never will,' Mrs Joyce snorted. 'It's just my weekly dose of harassment – courtesy of the Tyrant.'

'Lyd . . . My friend and I are on the moors,' Fran explained quickly. 'We need to see you. It's really important.'

'Where's Mike?' Mrs Joyce frowned.

Fran gave Lydia a worried look.

'I'm sorry Mrs Joyce, but the Tyrant has him in his mansion,' Fran replied.

'My God! What happened?'

'Mike took us to the Tyrant's mansion but they were waiting for us,' Fran explained.

'He did *what*?' Mrs Joyce exploded. 'Mike wouldn't . . . he *couldn't* be that stupid. Why did he do it?'

'It's a bit difficult to explain . . .'

'No, never mind. Not over the viewphone,' Mrs Joyce interrupted harshly. 'Mike . . .'

Lydia moved closer to Fran to see the viewphone's screen, but Mrs Joyce had her head bent, as if she didn't want anyone to see the pain she was going through. Fran pushed Lydia away as Mrs Joyce straightened up. Lydia frowned at her, wondering what was going on.

'Is he all right?' Mrs Joyce's face was now a mask. She could have been asking about the weather.

'When I last saw him he was,' Fran said.

'Mike won't tell the Tyrant anything . . .' Mrs Joyce seemed to be speaking more to herself than to Fran. She added with a bitter laugh, 'Daniel Henson really hates us, doesn't he?'

Lydia frowned at Fran. Although she couldn't see Mrs Joyce's face, she could still hear what was being said and instinctively she knew that Mrs Joyce wasn't talking about Daniel hating the whole town. She was talking about Daniel hating her and Mike specifically – Lydia was sure of it.

'Mrs Joyce, can we come to your house? Is it safe yet?' Fran asked again.

'No. You can't come here. The whole town is crawling with Guards and at least half of them are surrounding my house. I'll have to come to you. But don't worry, I'll get past them,' said Mrs Joyce.

'OK. We'll meet you in sector 4-M in twenty minutes,' said Fran.

She pressed a button and Mrs Joyce's face disappeared. Lydia turned towards the colours which lit up the dawn sky. White lightning flashed from the clouds, but there was no thunder and no rain.

Maybe it's an electrical storm? Lydia wondered. Whatever it was, it was still approaching.

'We'd better get going. We're meeting Mrs Joyce just outside the town so we'll have to be careful. And you'll have to change your clothes as soon as possible. The Guards will be looking for you and they know what you're wearing,' Fran said.

'Shouldn't we use the viewphone to warn Mrs Joyce that my brother knows about the tunnels?' asked Lydia.

'The Night Guards never enter the tunnels. They'd be far too easy to pick off,' said Fran. 'They'll use the tracker mobiles and Mrs Joyce can handle them.'

'Even so, shouldn't we tell Mrs Joyce . . . ?'

'It isn't safe. We can't say too much. We can't risk the Guards tapping into our transmission and tracking us down,' said Fran. 'Besides, that's not the reason I want us to meet up with Mrs Joyce.'

Lydia waited for Fran to continue. Worry and indecision flitted over Fran's face. She kicked at the ground beneath her feet. All of a sudden she couldn't look at Lydia.

'What's the matter?'

'Lydia, do you really want to help us?' Fran asked at last.

'Of course I do.'

'Even though Daniel is your brother?'

'What he's doing is wrong,' said Lydia without hesitation. 'I just want him to stop.'

'And what about returning to your own time?' said Fran.

'I don't know,' Lydia whispered. 'I'm afraid to go back if it means I'm going to die but . . . but I don't belong here either. I don't know what to do now.'

'Lydia, I know about the Collivale sports cup . . .'

'You do?'

Fran nodded. 'My mum told me before she died. She told me about it going missing and someone in her class being blamed for taking it, even though they hadn't. She never told me that person's name though. I didn't realize that it was Lydia Henson, the Tyrant's sister . . .'

Lydia frowned and waited for Fran to continue.

'Don't you understand?' Fran said urgently. 'I never realized that the person accused of taking the cup and Daniel's sister were one and the same person. That explains so much. Very few grown-ups know about this and those who do *never* talk about it.'

'I still don't understand.' Lydia shook her head.

Fran sighed. 'My middle name is Lydia, you know. My mum named me after you.'

'Did she? Did she really?' Lydia beamed like a Cheshire cat.

'Lydia, Mrs Joyce can tell you the truth about how the cup got into your locker . . .'

'How would she know anything about it?' Lydia asked.

'I think she should explain that, not me,' Fran replied.

Lydia huffed with exasperation. Fran was being so mysterious. It was driving her crazy! But it was obvious that something was troubling Fran deeply. Lydia put her arm around Fran's shoulders and smiled. Fran looked at her but didn't smile back.

'We'd better get going,' Fran said unhappily.

Lydia took one last look at the colours and lights flashing behind them, before she purposely turned her back and walked beside Fran across the moors.

They made their way in silence to sector 4-M which was about a mile away from where Lydia had first seen Fran. After a quick look around, Fran said, 'We'll be safer sitting down.'

Lydia sat down, still looking around. The moors held very little cover and rolled towards the horizon in all directions. Lydia imagined the Night Guards jumping out at them at any second but she knew that wasn't possible. There was no way the Night Guards could sneak up on them from any direction without one of them seeing the Guards first.

'Look over there.' Fran pointed.

Lydia did as directed. In the distance she could see two figures gliding along.

'The Night Guards patrol the moors each morning and evening,' explained Fran. 'They stand on their patrol boards and chat while they travel right round the perimeter of the moors. It's a five-hour journey but they don't have to take a step! That's what they call "patrolling"! Lucky for us that they're so lazy.'

Lydia watched them for a moment. The Guards were moving about on what looked like hovering skateboards. The boards made no sound, at least none that she could hear at this distance – and travelled about forty centimetres off the ground. It was so weird watching the Guards glide along silently.

'Are you OK?' asked Fran.

Lydia shrugged, then nodded. 'A bit tired, but I'll survive!' She turned to Fran. 'Now are you going to tell me what's the matter?'

Fran shook her head. She dug a hand into the earth beside her and let it trickle through her fingers.

'Lydia, my mum . . . my mum was always on your side. She knew you didn't take the sports cup. Mum always reckoned that Anne Turner did it, although she never managed to find any proof. She was working on Anne to try and prove it when you were killed,' said Fran.

'She was? She never told me that,' Lydia said.

'Mum said she tried, but you wouldn't listen. She told me that she tried to talk to you one time in a supermarket. And another time at school, just before the end of term.'

'I know about the supermarket. That happened . . . yesterday? The day before? Or thirty-seven years ago, depending on how you look at it!' Lydia realized ruefully. 'Frankie wanted to talk to me but I was too angry to listen. That's when she had her accident.'

'I wish you had listened to her,' Fran sighed.

'So do I,' Lydia agreed. 'I will do when I get back to my own time – *if I get back* . . .'

'Oh yeah! Not everything has happened yet,' Fran remembered. 'This is so peculiar.'

'Tell me about it!' Lydia said drily. 'You keep talking about things in the past tense, things that haven't even happened to me yet.'

'You two should pay more attention to who's sneaking up behind you!' Mrs Joyce's angry voice made Lydia jump. She and Fran sprang to their feet immediately.

'You scared us,' Fran breathed.

'Good! Then maybe next time, you'll chat and keep a look out at the same time,' said

Mrs Joyce, grabbing Fran by her arms and shaking her. Lydia tried to pull Fran away from Mrs Joyce's angry grasp. 'Is that how my son got caught? Is it? By chatting to you and not paying attention?'

'We were ambushed. As soon as Mike and I set foot out of the tunnel, the Tyr . . . Daniel's Night Guards were there waiting for us.' Lydia lowered her gaze when Mrs Joyce turned to look at her and kicked moodily at the dirt beneath her feet. 'It was a trap. They knew about the tunnels.'

Now that Lydia knew the Tyrant and her brother were definitely one and the same, she couldn't bear to call him by that name.

'Is that why you two dragged me all the way out here? To explain about my son?' Mrs Joyce's ice-cold voice chilled Lydia. 'What were you two doing there in the first place?'

'I asked for Mike's help. I wanted to see Daniel Henson,' Lydia admitted.

'And my fool of a son took you through the tunnels.' Mrs Joyce gave a bitter laugh.

Lydia looked up. Mrs Joyce gasped with shocked amazement. Lydia stared. Mrs Joyce looked just like . . . But it couldn't be . . . It just couldn't be.

'Mrs Joyce, *this* is why I asked you to come,' Fran said. 'Lydia's full name is Lydia Henson. Lydia Angela Henson.'

Mrs Joyce's head whipped around. She stared

at Fran, then turned back to Lydia, her eyes growing wider and wider.

'You can't be. I don't believe it. Lydia's dead,' Mrs Joyce whispered.

'No, she isn't. She was caught in a storm in 1995 and pitched into the future – to our time,' said Fran.

Mrs Joyce came closer until her face was only centimetres away from Lydia's. A mixture of disbelief and suspicion and wonder played across her face.

Lydia backed away, her heart slamming against her ribs. This was a grown woman. Mike's mum. A stranger. It couldn't be . . .

'Lydia, Mrs Joyce's name before she got married was Turner,' said Fran quietly. 'Her name is Anne. Anne Turner. She's the one who put the cup in your locker.'

Eighteen

Traitor!

'You mean . . . you mean you're Anne Turner?'

Lydia couldn't believe it. The person who had put the school sports cup in her locker. The one who had started all this. Anne . . .

'Lydia, what're you thinking?' Fran asked, uncertainly.

'This is some new trick of the Tyrant's. Fran, he's brainwashed you,' Mrs Joyce interrupted with conviction.

'Look at her, Mrs Joyce.' Fran pointed to Lydia. 'Just look at her.'

And all the time, Lydia studied the grown-up before her. The hair was cropped shorter, the face was slightly puffier, the lips a lot harder, the eyes a lot colder – but it was her.

'Anne Turner . . .'

And Mrs Anne Joyce was doing her fair share of scrutinizing as well. She shook her head slowly, then stopped.

'It really is you, isn't it?' Mrs Joyce said,

stunned. 'I don't know how or why, but it really is you.'

The air crackled with the tension between them. Lydia clenched her fists and forced her hands to remain by her sides. Her whole body remained stiff, as she fought to stop herself from flying at Anne.

'Why did you do it? Why did you put the cup in my locker?' asked Lydia, her face hard-set like ice.

Mrs Joyce laughed with self-derision. 'Would you believe because I was jealous. Fran's mum, Frankie, had always been my best friend – and then you arrived.'

So Bharti had been right . . .

'And how did you get the cup in my locker?' Lydia asked frostily.

She didn't see the grown-up woman standing in front of her. She saw Anne Turner, a spiteful twelve-year-old girl who had played a joke that had made her life a misery. Anne, who'd delighted in telling everyone that Lydia had deliberately caused Frankie's accident. Anne, whose 'jokes' were ultimately going to cost Lydia her life . . .

'I remember I left school, then doubled back and hid in the toilets. I knew you wouldn't take the cup.' Mrs Joyce closed her eyes as she spoke. 'I was so pleased with myself. No-one else realized that the lockers had backplates that were only held on with four screws. It was easy. I kept the cup in my locker until the next morning. After you'd arrived at school the following day, I just unscrewed the backplate with my screwdriver and put the cup in your locker. Then I left a message under the headmaster's door saying that if he wanted to find the school's sports cup, he should check all the lockers in the girls' cloakroom.'

'You did that?' Lydia was stunned.

Mrs Joyce nodded slowly, her expression contrite. 'My God, I was such a schemer!'

'That's why my brother hates you, isn't it?' Lydia realized. 'Because of what you did to me.'

'When the Tyrant first arrived here and I realized who he was, it . . . it felt as if I'd been kicked in the stomach. I tried to see him, to tell him how sorry . . . But he wouldn't even see me. Why should he?' Anne smiled with self-contempt. ' "Sorry!" – it's such a useless word . . . And bit by bit, he started taking over this town and making my life and my son's as miserable as possible. I loathe him for that,' Anne said, bitterness twisting her face. 'For dragging my son into this.'

'Because of what you did, you ruined the lives of everyone in my family,' Lydia pointed out coldly.

They watched each other like opponents sizing up one another in a boxing ring.

'And why did you tell everyone that I'd pushed Frankie in the car-park?' Lydia asked, her eyes blazing.

'I thought you'd pushed her, I really did,' Mrs Joyce replied quietly. 'From where I was, I saw your hand out and Frankie falling. It was only when Frankie woke up and said what'd really happened that I realized my mistake.'

'You wanted to believe I'd pushed her,' Lydia countered bitterly.

Mrs Joyce didn't deny it. She reached out a tentative hand towards Lydia's face, then dropped her arm to her side without touching Lydia.

'Are you . . . are you a ghost?' Mrs Joyce asked.

Lydia was about to deny it, but then she said, 'If a ghost is someone who's out of place and out of time then I guess maybe I am.'

'D'you want to know something funny,' Mrs Joyce said sadly. 'When we all got back to school after Christmas and heard what had happened to you, Frankie just looked at me. I remember she didn't say a word, she just looked. After that she never said another word to me. So I lost my best friend anyway. I didn't want to share her with you and as a result I ended up losing her completely. And then when she married Shaun, he didn't want anything to do with me either – at least not until the Tyrant arrived. Then we had to be on the same side.'

Lydia glanced at Fran who was watching her closely. Mrs Joyce turned to Fran as well.

'When Mike and Fran became good friends I

thought . . . it was as if what I'd done in the past was being made right . . .'

'I knew you were the one who put the sports cup in my locker. I just knew it.' Lydia shook her head. 'If only I'd been able to prove it.'

'You never did,' Mrs Joyce said. 'I remember that before the end of term, you pushed me into our classroom one lunchtime to get me alone and confront me. I think you just wanted to hear me say it, to hear me admit the truth – just once. I was so angry I blurted everything out, to gloat. So you always knew I'd done it but no-one believed you.'

Lydia didn't say a word. She studied Mrs Joyce, her face a mask.

'We'd better get back to town. There's a lot to do if we're going to launch a surprise attack on my brother,' she said at last.

'You're still going to help us?' Fran asked.

'Of course. I know where Mike is so I'll be responsible for trying to get him out,' Lydia replied.

'We'll have to go across the moors and through the town,' Fran frowned.

'Can't we use the tunnels?' Lydia asked.

'We'd better not. They're not as safe during the daytime. We'd be too easy to ambush,' Fran explained. 'During the night it's the other way around. *We* rule the night.'

Lydia nodded but said nothing.

'I'm so sorry, Lydia,' Mrs Joyce said. She tried to put a hand on Lydia's shoulder but Lydia pulled away.

'We'd better get going,' Lydia said. 'We've got a lot to do.'

All the way back to town, Lydia was aware of the wary looks Fran kept directing at her. She knew that Fran would've loved to know what she was thinking. Lydia smiled without any real humour. How could Fran know what she was thinking when Lydia herself didn't even know?

'Mrs Joyce, you should walk directly in front of us and I'll walk on the outside, beside Lydia. Lydia, make sure you walk in perfect step with me. That's the only way we're going to get away with this. If this works the Guards in the camp will only pick up two images on their mobile radar and gate monitors instead of three. Of course, this is all academic if there are actually Guards by the gates on look-out. Let's hope we're lucky.'

'We need to get off the street as soon as possible,' Mrs Joyce said, worried.

Fran agreed. They walked slowly past the Night Guards' camp. Lydia could see the beads of sweat trickling down Fran's forehead but she didn't even raise a hand to wipe them away.

'Across the street. We're being watched,' Fran whispered.

A Guard directly opposite had turned around and was now watching them.

'Stop walking, or they'll see that there's three of us,' Fran urged.

They all stopped walking. Mrs Joyce turned around and pretended to start a conversation with Fran. Lydia held her breath.

Turn away . . . Oh please, turn away . . .

'You two! Let me see some ID.' A Guard called out from directly opposite.

Mrs Joyce turned around and slowly they all carried on walking.

'You two! Didn't you hear me?' the Guard shouted.

Without warning, Lydia pushed Fran out of the way and ran across the street to the Guard.

'Help me! Help me! I'm the one Daniel Henson wants,' Lydia screamed out.

She ran straight to the startled Guard who grabbed her by her arm.

'Security to sector 2-R. Repeat! Security to sector 2-R.' The Guard spoke into the transmitter strapped to his arm.

'Lydia, you traitor!' Fran yelled.

Lydia turned back, just in time to see Fran's look of loathing before she and Mrs Joyce raced off in different directions. The Guard released Lydia and pointed his laser-gun at Mrs Joyce.

'No!' Lydia knocked his arm up, spoiling his aim.

Furiously, the Guard swung around to her, his gun levelled straight at her head. Lydia froze. She didn't even dare to blink. Time slowed down so that every second lasted a lifetime. Lydia watched as the Night Guard's finger tightened slowly but surely on the trigger. And this time, she knew that the gun wasn't set on stun.

Nineteen

You're Still My Sister

A blast came out of nowhere and knocked the Night Guard flying up into the air. He fell in a crumpled heap about a metre away from Lydia. She stared at him, too afraid to even blink.

'Are you all right? Did he hurt you?'

Lydia was turned around to face Daniel Henson who was surrounded by bodyguards on all sides.

'Is . . . is he dead?' Lydia looked back at the Night Guard who hadn't moved.

'No, he's just stunned,' Daniel said scornfully. 'But I would've killed him if he'd harmed a hair on your head.'

Lydia took a quick step back, away from Daniel. He saw it and his lips tightened to an angry slash across his face.

'I don't know you.' Lydia shook her head. 'And I don't like you. My brother wouldn't hurt anyone. He was funny and kind and he didn't even like stepping on ants. You're not my brother.'

'Lydia, things happen which change us – all of us,' Daniel said quietly.

Lydia looked up at her brother. 'Not that much, Danny. You shouldn't have let anything, not even my death, change you that much.'

'You'd have done exactly the same for me, if our positions had been reversed.'

'No way!' Lydia denied vehemently. 'I wouldn't have turned into a bully and a tyrant.'

A very peculiar smile played over Daniel's face.

'Lyddy, you sound very sure of that.' Even though he was still smiling, Daniel's voice was tinged with something else. Regret? Sadness? But then Lydia realized something else.

Lyddy . . . He'd called her Lyddy. And what he'd said . . . It'd only just sunk in.

'You . . . you believe me? You believe that I'm your sister?' Lydia asked, amazed.

'Of course. I have proof now,' said Daniel.

'What proof?'

'The wound on your arm.'

'I don't understand.'

'You have a wound on your arm, don't you?' asked Daniel. 'It's shaped like an S on its side, like a Sidewinder snake.'

'So?' Lydia asked.

Daniel nodded. 'I think it's time you learnt the truth, Lydia. Come with me.'

Lydia followed Daniel to his private car. She climbed into the back next to her brother but made sure not to touch him. She didn't want any part of his hatred or need for revenge to rub off on her. It was only when she sat down in the soft, comfortable seats that she realized just how tired she was. When was the last time she'd been asleep? When was the last time she'd eaten? Not that she could eat much anyway. She was too tired. One of Daniel's bodyguards got into the driver's seat and started the car. Lydia looked out of the window, holding her breath as the car took off vertically before it flew like an arrow over the houses below.

'Only four of us in this town – besides the Night Guards – have private air cars. They're very expensive to buy and to run,' said Daniel. 'Plus I'm the one who has to authorize the car permits.'

Lydia frowned at him but said nothing.

Daniel shook his head and smiled with wonder. 'I still can't believe you're here. It's a miracle. I don't understand . . . but enough of that. There's plenty of time for explanations later. Lyddy, there's so much I want to tell you, so much . . .'

But Lydia hardly heard him. She struggled to keep her eyes open but it was no good. Seconds later she was fast asleep.

'Lyddy, wake up.'

Lydia opened her eyes slowly. Daniel's face was smiling down at her. She sat up slowly and looked around. She was on a sofa, back in Daniel's mansion.

'Here. Eat this.'

Lydia looked down at the plate Daniel was carrying. A small but thick foil wrapper sat in the middle of the plate.

'What is it?'

'A synthetic meat sandwich. What flavour of meat do you want?' asked Daniel.

'I don't understand . . .'

'Ham? Beef? Chicken?'

'I'd like ham,' Lydia said doubtfully.

Daniel put the plate with its foil wrapper into what looked like a small microwave oven. He pressed a couple of buttons. The oven beeped and whirred for a few seconds. Daniel opened the door again and took out the plate. Thick slices of ham spilled out between two thick slices of brown bread. Daniel handed over the plate.

Lydia picked up the sandwich and examined it doubtfully. Synthetic meat . . . That didn't sound too appetizing at all! Daniel laughed at the expression on her face.

'Go on! Try it,' he urged.

Lydia bit gingerly into the sandwich. It was delicious! The moment she started to chew, she realized just how hungry she was. It took all her will-power not to wolf it down.

'Where's Mike?' Lydia asked, between bites. 'Is he OK?'

'Yes, of course.'

'You . . . you won't hurt him.'

'No.'

'Are you sure?'

'I promise,' Daniel said.

'How long have I been asleep?'

'A couple of hours.'

Daniel sat down next to Lydia and waited for her to finish her sandwich. Lydia avoided his gaze. All kinds of other questions about the future came into her head now. Like what had happened to their mum and dad?

'Mum and Dad . . .' Lydia began slowly. 'Are they . . . are they still alive?'

After a brief but definite pause, Daniel slowly shook his head.

'How did . . . ? No, don't tell me.' Lydia didn't want to know what had happened to their parents. The phrase 'a little knowledge is a dangerous thing . . .' spun round in her head. There were so many things she wanted to ask. A whole thirty-seven years worth of questions – like were there any tigers or rhinos or elephants or whales left in the world? What had happened to London and the government and the Houses of Parliament? Were there any time machines? Was *Grange Hill* still on the telly? Could manned Earth spaceships visit Mars yet? Had aliens from other planets visited Earth? Why was everyone so afraid? What *had* happened to their mum and dad . . . ? What had happened to Daniel? Was there any way that she could change time to stop the motorway accident in 1995 . . . ?

'D'you want another sandwich?' Daniel smiled.

Lydia shook her head. She looked up at him. He looked more like the brother she knew now. Somehow his face seemed softer, less harsh.

'Has something happened?' Lydia asked.

Had the Resistance already attacked while Lydia had been asleep? Was that why Daniel was smiling? Because he'd beaten them?

'Like what?' Daniel asked.

'Why're you being so kind to me all of a sudden?' Lydia said, bluntly.

'You're my sister. This is a really strange situation but you're still my sister.' Daniel shrugged. 'Lyddy, I want you to know that no matter how things look to you at the moment, I do care about you. I'm doing all of this for you.'

'If that's true, then will you stop hounding everyone in this town if I ask you?' Lydia asked. 'I don't want you to do it any more. I want you to stop. If you started this for me, you'll stop for me.'

'I can't do that, Lyddy,' Daniel sighed.

'Why not?' Lydia asked unhappily.

Daniel didn't answer.

'I didn't understand why I was brought here, to the future, but I do now. It's to stop you. To get you to change your mind. Please, Daniel. I'm asking you to stop,' Lydia pleaded.

'Come with me.' Daniel beckoned.

Lydia stood up and followed Daniel out of the room and across the hall. They went upstairs in silence and then along the long, narrow landing to the room at the far end of the corridor. After a brief look at Lydia, Daniel knocked at the door.

'Come in,' a woman's voice summoned.

The voice sent Lydia's heart racing. All at once, her palms were sweaty and her heart was pounding. Surprised, Lydia realized that she was actually frightened. But why?

Daniel opened the door. Lydia followed him in.

The room was cold, gloomy. A single lamp at the other end of the room gave off the only light. It took several seconds for Lydia's eyes to adjust to the darkness. This room was filled with books like the one downstairs but, unlike the one downstairs, this room smelt lonely and dark. That was the only way she could describe it. A couple of chairs decorated the room. The floor was polished wood and in the wall adjacent to the door was an unlit fireplace.

With a start Lydia realized that what she had first believed to be a long shadow in the corner of the room was actually a person. Someone was standing there watching her – an old-looking woman leaning heavily on a walking-stick, her face shrouded in shadow. The prickling all over Lydia's body was back with a vengeance and her blood roared in her ears.

The woman started walking towards her. Her stick made a dull thud as it hit the wooden floor with each step. She was wearing a long dark skirt which reached down to the floor and a white shirt buttoned up to her neck. With each step, the lamplight stole slowly up her body until only her face was still in darkness.

Even when Lydia realized that she was holding her breath, she still didn't dare to release it. She glanced at Daniel. He, too, was watching the woman as if he couldn't tear his eyes away. Lydia turned back to the woman, who was once again moving forward. Then all at once Lydia could clearly see her face and her breath came out in a horrified gasp.

The woman's face was horrible – not so much her face as her eyes. They seemed to burn right through Lydia's body. The woman's face was all deep creases in her forehead and permanently turned-down lips. A scar ran from her right eye across to her right ear, but that wasn't what made the old woman ugly. It was her expression, full of bitterness and pain and overwhelming hatred. She stared at Lydia and, not once, not once did she blink.

Lydia moved closer towards Daniel. She was trembling and couldn't stop. She wanted to close her eyes and turn away from the woman before her but she couldn't. It was as if an invisible clamp had locked onto her head and was stopping her from looking anywhere but at this old woman.

The woman made her slow, painful way over to Lydia to stop directly in front of her. Without a word she unbuttoned her left shirt sleeve and pushed it up past her elbow to her shoulder. Then she turned her arm slightly so that Lydia could take a closer look. Lydia's heart leapt. The old woman had a smooth, deep-brown scar on the slightly lighter-brown skin of her arm. The scar was shaped like an S on its side, like a Sidewinder snake.

Lydia looked down at her own arm. She unbuttoned her left shirt sleeve cuff and pushed it up. Under the medical staples, beneath the slight smear of blood where the wound had started to seep again, was the identically-shaped scar. Lydia's was a fresher wound and it hadn't yet healed, but there was no doubt about it. The scar was the same shape and in exactly the same place.

With horror, Lydia looked into the woman's face.

'Hello, Lydia,' the woman said.

'No, it can't be . . .' Lydia looked up at Daniel but he looked away, unable to meet her eyes.

Lydia shook her head. It couldn't be, it just couldn't. It was impossible and yet . . . Lydia stretched out her hand and touched the scar on the old woman's arm. The scar was warm and smooth, unlike the skin surrounding it. Lydia's arm fell slowly to her side. The scar, just like the old woman, was very real.

'I didn't die in a car crash . . .' Lydia whispered, totally shocked. 'You're . . . you're *me*!'

Twenty

A Lesson In Hatred

Lydia couldn't take her eyes off the bitter old woman standing before her. It was her, years and years into the future. *It was her* . . . Lydia turned to Daniel. 'You lied to me. You said I died in a car crash. How could you do that? *How could you?*'

'He only told you what everyone else was told,' the woman interrupted. 'We *were* in a car crash a week before my thirteenth birthday. I was critically injured. And even when I did eventually recover, for a while everyone thought I'd never walk again.' The old woman paused and looked pointedly down at her walking stick. 'By the time I was able to leave hospital, our parents decided never to return to Tarwich. So we moved back down to London.'

'But why did you let everyone think you'd died?' Lydia asked, bewildered.

'A part of me *did* die in the accident,' the woman said softly. 'The part of me that believed in other people. That's why I had the dates put on my memorial. So I'd never forget. I don't trust or rely on anyone. The monument was built to attest to the truth of that.'

Lydia looked from the woman to Daniel and back again.

'It's you!' she said, dumbfounded. '*You're* the one who's making everyone's life miserable in this town. Everyone thinks it's Danny, but he's only doing it for you.'

'Danny's doing what he knows is right,' said the woman.

Lydia looked up at her brother.

'But it's not right, Daniel,' Lydia said urgently. 'Dad always says that two wrongs don't make a right.'

'The people of this town are getting exactly what they deserve,' Daniel replied.

'Then why do you look so unhappy?' Lydia asked. 'What're you getting out of it, if it makes you just as miserable as everyone else in Tarwich?'

'Hensonville,' Old Lydia corrected softly. 'This is my town now. Everyone and everything in it belongs to me.'

'You can't own people. You can buy all the houses and the roads and the buildings, but you'll never *own* the people here. You can't own how they think and feel. And they hate you. Is that really what you want?' Arguing with Old Lydia was like beating her head against a brick wall, but Lydia had to try. She had to make her older self see sense.

'Enough! I don't remember being like you at all.' Old Lydia shook her head. 'I can't remember ever being that . . . naive.'

'How old are you?' Lydia whispered.

'Forty-nine,' Old Lydia replied. 'Going on one hundred and forty-nine.'

And it was true. The woman looked a lot older than forty-nine. Her eyes showed that what she looked like outside was just a reflection of what she was inside – as cold and hard as permafrost.

Lydia's head was spinning. She didn't die in a car crash, after all. But as she looked up at the woman before her, Lydia realized it wasn't that simple. She hadn't died, but she'd turned into something she didn't recognize. Something she didn't *want* to recognize.

'Danny, don't listen to her. She's wrong. She's . . . evil . . .'

'You and I are the same, Lydia. Don't forget that,' Old Lydia said. 'You hate the people in this town just as much as I do. You're going to grow up into me.'

'No way. Never,' Lydia denied vigorously. 'I'll never become you. I'm going back to my own time and I'm going to change the future.'

'You can't. I exist, just as much as you do,' Old Lydia scoffed.

'But . . . but I'm changing things already – just by being here. I must be.' Lydia spoke her thoughts out loud.

Lydia looked up just in time to see the look which passed between her older self and Daniel.

'What is it? There's still something you're not telling me,' Lydia confronted them.

Silence.

'I want to go home. Now. How do I get back to my own time?' Lydia asked her older self.

'I don't know,' Old Lydia admitted after a long pause.

Lydia stared at her. 'You must know. Just tell me how you got back when you were my age.'

'I never came into the future when I was your age. This never happened to me,' said Old Lydia.

'I don't understand. Then how did you get the scar on your arm?' Lydia asked.

'On the moors – when I got lost,' said Old Lydia. 'I can't remember much about it, but I always thought I must've fallen on some broken glass or maybe been kicked by a moor pony or something . . .'

'But how is that possible?' Lydia asked. 'How can something happen to me that hasn't happened to you?'

'We don't know,' Daniel admitted. 'I wish we did. Maybe the past, present and future all exist simultaneously so each can be reached and each can have an effect on the other? I don't know.'

'Then this future isn't for definite?' Lydia frowned.

Daniel shook his head. 'I don't believe it is – no. Maybe this is just one possible future. I believe there are many others.'

From the expression on his face, Lydia knew that Daniel was aware of what she was asking. She wanted to know if by going back to 1995 she could change the future. Could she change the year 2032 AD as Daniel and Old Lydia knew it and as she had seen it?

'I think I understand,' Lydia said slowly. 'But how does that help me? How do I get back?'

'You said you were on the moors in the middle of a storm when you were knocked unconscious. Maybe the storm had something to do with it,' Daniel suggested.

The storm . . . The swirling colours and the lightning flashes . . . That had to be it!

'There's an electrical storm over the moors now,' Lydia remembered. 'That must be how I get back to my own time.'

'How?' asked Daniel.

'I don't know, but I have to go back there. And this time I have to go into the storm instead of away from it. The moors are where it all started,' said Lydia.

'You're not going anywhere,' said Old Lydia silkily.

Lydia stared up at Old Lydia.

'What're you talking about?' she asked. 'I have to get back to my own time. I don't belong here.'

'You're not leaving this house until you tell us who the leaders of the Resistance are and when they're planning to attack us,' said Old Lydia.

Lydia couldn't believe her ears. Here she was with a chance – albeit slim – to change this . . . this nightmare, and all Old Lydia cared about were the names of the leaders of the Resistance.

'Don't you understand? I have to get back to the moors,' Lydia pleaded. 'The storm might fizzle out and disappear at any time. Then I'd be stuck here.'

'Why should I care about that?' Old Lydia raised an eyebrow. 'You're not going anywhere until you tell me what I want to know. Then we'll make sure that all the members of the Resistance are dealt with.'

'Daniel, you'll help me, won't you?' Lydia appealed to her brother. 'I can change all this – I know I can.'

'And if we don't want it changed?' asked Old Lydia, feigning patience.

'You don't mean that . . .' Lydia thought for one brief moment that she'd misheard, but the expression on Old Lydia's face told her otherwise.

'What're you so afraid of?' Exasperation made Lydia's voice grow louder and more desperate by the second. 'If I go back to my own time and I

fail then nothing changes here. But if I succeed
. . . Danny, *please*.'

'Don't you see what this means, Lydia?' Daniel
spoke to the old woman before him. 'If we *can* get
her back to 1995, she might be able to change the
future – for both of us. We won't have to live like
this any more.'

Old Lydia stared at her brother as if he'd lost
his mind.

'You want to help the people of this town?' Old
Lydia scorned.

'No. No way. But I do want to help *us*. You and
me. That's all I've ever cared about.'

'Don't let that one . . .' Old Lydia pointed a
disdainful finger at her younger self. 'Don't let her
make you forget why we're doing this.'

'I haven't forgotten, Lydia. And I never will. But
I'm getting tired.' Danny sighed. 'When we crush
the Resistance, within months a new one will
spring up in its place.'

'And we'll crush them as well,' Old Lydia said
at once.

'And then what? Is this really how you want to
spend the rest of your life?' asked Daniel.

'There is nothing else.'

'But there might be – if we help Lydia to get
back to 1995 and she changes her present. There
must be something more than this. And we've got
absolutely nothing to lose.'

The old woman's eyes took on an icy glint as

she looked from Lydia to Daniel and back again. Lydia glared at the old woman and hated what she saw. Old Lydia was what she'd let herself become. She'd grown bitter and twisted, both inside and out, and here was the end result. Old Lydia leaned more heavily on her walking-stick as she continued to scrutinize her brother.

Lydia remembered what she'd heard about the motorway accident. But it wasn't the town's fault. A lorry had ploughed into them. Daniel had told her that. More than ever, Lydia longed to get back to her own time. She knew with absolute certainty that once she got back, even if she couldn't prove that she didn't take the Collivale sports cup, she would *never* turn into the embittered, old battleaxe who stood in front of her. Never in a million years.

'When do the Resistance plan to attack us?' asked Old Lydia.

'I don't know,' Lydia said coldly.

'Yes, you do. You were spotted by an aerial probe with Anne Joyce and Fran Lucas on the moors this morning.'

'We were just out walking,' Lydia said.

'Anne Joyce is the leader of the Resistance, isn't she?' Old Lydia's lips twisted.

Lydia realized that this was the old woman's version of a smile. She obviously hadn't smiled in so long that she'd forgotten how.

'I don't know what you're talking about,' Lydia replied.

'Answer my question.' Old Lydia abandoned all attempt to be pleasant.

'I'm not saying a word to you,' Lydia hissed.

Old Lydia grabbed her by her arm, her bony fingers like pincers.

'Ow!' Lydia grimaced.

Old Lydia had purposely grabbed her over her wound.

'Lydia, let her go,' Daniel told the old woman.

'Not until she answers my questions,' said Old Lydia. 'Daniel, go and get Anne Joyce's brat.'

Daniel looked at both Lydias uncertainly.

'Do as I say,' ordered Old Lydia.

Daniel left the room without another word.

Old Lydia thrust Lydia down into a chair and immediately bent over her so that Lydia couldn't get up.

'You are me,' said Old Lydia, softly. 'You think as I think. You feel as I feel. Just remember what this town did to you. How they all called you a thief and made your life a misery. How they all blamed you for Frances Weldon being knocked over. Even when Frances woke up and said it was an accident, most of the town didn't believe it. Just remember the phone calls and the paint and the hate mail. The people here made us what we are. They owe us.'

'But you didn't have to let them turn you into . . . into a monster. *You* made yourself what you are, not the people of this town,' Lydia argued.

'And I'm not like you – not any more. I don't hate anyone.'

'No?' asked Old Lydia.

'No!' Lydia said adamantly.

'We'll see.' Old Lydia smiled.

A noise on the landing outside had Old Lydia straightening up. Lydia jumped out of her chair immediately and put as much space as possible between her and Old Lydia.

The door burst open and Mike fell into the room, thrown in by a Night Guard who waited for Daniel to enter the room before he began to shut the door behind him.

'You! Stay here,' Old Lydia commanded.

The Night Guard walked over to Old Lydia and stood by her side. Daniel leaned against the closed door, without saying a word.

'Lydia, are you OK? I thought . . . I'd hoped you'd got away.' Mike got to his feet and went over to Lydia.

'I'm fine. Are you OK, Mike?' Lydia asked.

Mike nodded.

'Save your concern,' Old Lydia said with contempt.

Mike turned to her, his head held high. 'Who are you?' he asked arrogantly.

Lydia couldn't help smiling at Mike. She admired his courage.

'Lydia, why don't you tell him that?' Old Lydia taunted.

'She's a mean, spiteful, old trout,' Lydia retorted.

His eyes watchful, Mike regarded Old Lydia suspiciously.

'I'm Lydia Henson,' the old woman stated. 'The real ruler of this town.'

'But . . . but you're dead,' Mike whispered, aghast.

'Ah! I see your mother *has* told you about me,' Old Lydia said with satisfaction.

'Please let him go,' Lydia pleaded.

Old Lydia turned to the Guard. Her words rang out, cold and clear.

'I'm going to ask . . . this girl a question. If she doesn't answer,' Old Lydia pointed to Mike, 'kill him.'

'You can't do that,' Lydia said, appalled.

'D'you know whose son this is?' Old Lydia asked.

'He's Anne's son,' Lydia replied. 'I know that already.'

'Then you should want him dead.' Old Lydia's eyes glinted.

'I only came here with Lydia so I'd get a chance to kill the Tyrant,' said Mike fiercely. 'But now I'll make sure I get both of you.'

'Shut up, child. You're as repulsive as your mother,' said Old Lydia. 'And far from killing me, you're the one who's about to breathe his last if I don't get what I want.'

Lydia turned to Daniel. He wasn't looking at her. He was looking at Old Lydia. Looking at her as if he was only just seeing her for the first time.

'Now tell me what I want to know. When do the Resistance plan to attack us?' Old Lydia asked.

Lydia looked from the Night Guard to Old Lydia. She had to do something – anything. *But what?*

'Answer my question,' Old Lydia ordered.

'I don't know,' Lydia whispered.

Old Lydia turned to the Night Guard.

'Kill him,' she said.

The Guard levelled his laser gun at Mike.

'No!' Lydia called out.

Then everything happened at once. Lydia stepped in front of Mike and the room was suddenly full of laser light. Lydia froze. She looked down at her chest, wondering why she couldn't feel any pain. A shadow passed over her and when Lydia looked up, Daniel was standing beside her, a small laser-gun in his hand. Lydia could see the sprawled-out body of the Night Guard in front of Old Lydia.

'Lydia, you're my sister and I love you, but enough is enough,' Daniel told Old Lydia. 'I want something better for us than this.' Daniel nodded in Lydia's direction. 'She can go back and change things and, like I said, we have nothing to lose. I'm tired of living with all this hatred.'

'You traitor! I thought you were on my side,' Old Lydia said bitterly.

'DON'T YOU DARE SAY THAT TO ME!' Daniel exploded.

He shook with rage, his hands clenched at his sides as he tried to regain control of himself.

'I've made everyone in this town suffer because I was on your side. I've never had a life of my own because I was on your side. But it doesn't have to be like this. We have a chance to put things right and I'm going to take it.'

'Over my dead body,' said Old Lydia.

'It'll be over your heavily stunned body if that's what it takes,' Daniel replied quietly, raising his gun.

Old Lydia stared at him. Whatever answer she'd been expecting, it hadn't been that.

'Lydia, for years I've done as you've asked because you're my sister. We made money, we bought this town, we . . .' Daniel's lips clamped together as he bit back what he was going to say. Moments passed before he continued. 'Whilst it was all we had, it was enough. But now we have the chance for something *more*. Can't you see that?'

'I don't care about that,' Old Lydia replied bitterly. '*Now* is all I care about. Crushing the rebellion and punishing every member of the Resistance is all I care about. I'll destroy them all – except for Anne Turner. I want her to suffer.

And delivering her son's dead body to her doorstep will be only the beginning.'

The twelve-year-old Lydia shook her head as she watched her older self spew out all her poison like vomit. It was like watching a total stranger.

And a stranger is all you are, and all you'll ever be, Lydia thought with fiery determination.

Daniel turned away from the old woman. 'Lydia, you and Mike go downstairs and wait for me in the hall. We're going to the moors,' he said.

'What about her?' Mike pointed at the old woman.

'I can't get through to her any more. No-one can,' Daniel said, dejected.

Lydia took one final look at her older self. She memorized every down-turned line, every bitter crease. She studied the acid look of anger and hatred and promised herself that she'd never forget it. Ever.

'Come on, Mike,' Lydia said.

They left the room and ran downstairs.

'Quick! We've got to get out of here before the Tyrant catches up with us,' Mike urged. He grabbed Lydia's arm and headed for the front door.

'No, Mike,' Lydia said, pulling away. 'We have to stay here. We must wait.'

'No. He'll be down here at any moment,' Mike argued.

'I'm staying here,' Lydia repeated firmly.

'But . . .'

Daniel came down the stairs. At Lydia's enquiring glance, he said, 'Don't worry. All I've done is lock my sister and the Guard in that room. By the time Lydia manages to get out of the room via one of the secret passages, we'll be on our way. Now let's get going.'

Daniel threw open the front doors – and there stood Mike's mother, Anne, and the others of the Resistance. At least fifty people stood before them – men, women and children. With a triumphant laugh, they raised their laser guns higher, pointing them straight at Daniel and Lydia.

Twenty-One

To The Moors

Lydia didn't dare move. One blink in the wrong place and it'd be her last. Amongst those before her, Lydia saw Fran's dad. And by his side was Fran, who glared at her with very recognizable contempt.

'Put your hands up – both of you,' Mrs Joyce said.

Frightened, Lydia looked up at her brother. 'Please, you don't understand . . .' Lydia began.

'Oh we understand all right,' said Fran's dad. 'You tried to betray us to the Tyrant but we got here before he could summon his security police against us.'

'That's not true,' Lydia cried. 'Mike, tell them that's not true.'

Mike looked from Lydia to Daniel and back again. Uncertainty warred with his hatred of the Tyrant.

'Mike, are you OK? Did he hurt you?' his mum asked anxiously.

Mike's expression cleared. He stepped away from Daniel and Lydia to join his mum.

'You arrived just in time, Mum,' said Mike. 'I told Lydia to make a break for it but she wanted to stay here with him.'

Lydia blinked back the tears as she listened. All the faces, all the expressions, the feelings – they were mirror images of Old Lydia's upstairs.

'Fran, please – you know why I wanted to see Daniel. Tell them. Tell them why.' Lydia couldn't believe this was happening. Not now she was so close . . .

'You mean your story about coming from the year 1995?' Fran scoffed. 'I'm ashamed to say I actually believed you until Mrs Joyce and I realized what you were up to. You were sent by the Tyrant to infiltrate us, weren't you? The whole time I thought we were friends and all you wanted was to find out who the leaders of the Resistance were and when we were going to launch our attack against him.' Fran pointed to Daniel.

Lydia was speechless. Every word she wanted to scream in denial faded to nothing in her mouth.

'I don't need the help of a girl or anyone else come to that to crush this mob,' Daniel scorned.

'Yeah? Then how come you're the ones with your hands up and not us?' Fran's father said.

The mob around him laughed and cheered and whistled.

'Let her go. She has nothing to do with this.' Daniel pointed at Lydia.

'You expect us to believe that,' Mrs Joyce mocked. 'Take them inside and tie them up. We'll use them as hostages until we've taken care of the security police and the Night Guards.'

'They'll shoot you on sight,' Daniel said.

'Oh yeah? Where are the security police who're supposed to be protecting your precious mansion? D'you see them? 'Cause I don't,' sneered Mrs Joyce. 'We'll get rid of all your other Guards just as easily as we got rid of them.'

Daniel looked around the mob, but said nothing. Lydia wrapped her arms around herself so that no-one would see how much she was trembling. She moved a step closer to Daniel. Over the heads of the mob, through the branches and leaves of the trees in the wood, she could see a pink and orange sky towards the horizon. That was where she had to get to. Lydia was more convinced of that than ever before. But how? *How?*

'Take them inside,' Mrs Joyce commanded.

Fifteen minutes later, Lydia and Daniel were sitting in two chairs placed back to back and tied up tighter than Christmas parcels. They were back in Daniel's living room, and even though it wasn't cold, a fire blazed in the fireplace.

Fran's dad and two others came into the room. 'We've checked the entire house. There's an unconscious Night Guard upstairs and we caught two more security guards eating in the kitchen. That's it,' said Fran's dad.

Lydia turned to Daniel to ask about Old Lydia but a warning nudge from his elbow brought her to her senses. Mrs Joyce studied the two people tied up in front of her.

'OK then. You, you and you – you're responsible for the Tyrant and this traitor,' said Mrs Joyce, indicating Daniel and Lydia. 'If they so much as breathe the wrong way, you know what to do. The rest of us are off to the Night Guards' camp. This is it, people! Nothing can stop us now!'

With a great cheer, all the members of the Resistance left the room except for Fran's dad, a bald man and a tall woman, neither of whom Lydia recognized. Lydia heard the trudge of many footsteps out in the hall and then the front door slam shut. Lydia's captors each swaggered around the room, directing mocking looks at Daniel. Yet for all their jokes and laughter at Daniel's expense, Lydia saw that they were still careful not to come too close to him.

Lydia felt her brother's fingers pull at the plastic ropes around her wrists. She flexed her wrist and positioned her hands where she hoped none of the grown-ups in the room would see what Daniel was doing. The ropes were cutting into her wrists and each time Daniel pulled at them, it made them cut deeper but Lydia forced herself to bear the pain.

'Look at all these books. They're priceless,' said the woman in disgust.

'The rest of us have to make do with book-viewers and he's got more books than the town museum,' said the bald man.

'Danny, what're we going to do?' Lydia whispered.

'Shut up, you two. No talking,' snapped the woman.

'Huh! My Fran's never even seen a real book – like the rest of the kids in this town,' sniffed Fran's dad. 'And look at all this, going to waste.'

'I don't mind, Dad,' Fran began.

Lydia hadn't known that Fran was in the room until she heard her voice.

'Well, I do,' Fran's dad interrupted. 'Nothing compares to the smell and look and *feel* of real books. To be able to turn real pages . . .'

'But I can do that now,' said Fran. 'I just press the "forward-a-page" or "back-a-page" key. And I can search for a character's name or any word in the book and the book-viewer will put me on that page. And it's got an in-built dictionary. And if I don't feel like reading, my book-viewer will read the book out to me. The book-viewers are ten times better than real books!'

'No, they're not,' Fran's dad argued.

'But . . .'

'I said no, they're not – and that's all there is to it!' snapped Fran's dad.

And all the while Daniel's fingers worked on the knot which secured Lydia's wrists.

'Dad, you should go and see what else the Tyrant's got in his house that we can use,' said Fran slowly. 'Once the others get back here, it'll be every person for themselves.'

'And what about our prisoners?' the bald man asked.

'I'll look after them. They're not going anywhere,' Fran replied.

Lydia tried to turn her head to see Fran but she was bound too tightly. She wished she could just see Fran's face.

'We're not leaving you alone with those two, especially the Tyrant,' frowned Fran's dad.

'I'll be fine. If they try anything at all, I'll shoot first and ask questions later,' said Fran.

'It'll probably be our only chance to get what we want from the Tyrant's house before the others come back . . .' said the woman.

'Hhmm! OK then,' agreed Fran's dad. 'But Fran, just yell if they start anything.'

'Don't worry, Dad. I will,' Fran replied.

Lydia listened to the sound of three sets of footsteps retreating.

'Fran, is that you?' Lydia whispered.

No reply, but Lydia was sure someone was still in the room with them. *Please let it be Fran . . .*

'Fran, listen to me,' Lydia twisted her head this way and that but she could see no-one. 'Fran, I wasn't lying to you – I swear I wasn't. I'm from 1995. I don't belong here. *Please.* You must help me to get back. I can stop all this. I can *change* it. Then maybe even your mum Frankie wouldn't have to die. Fran . . . Fran . . .'

A single pair of footsteps sounded on the wooden floor, coming closer and closer. Lydia turned her head as far as she could but she still couldn't see a thing. Daniel's fingers stilled on Lydia's ropes. At last Fran came into view, carrying a knife with a long blade in her hand. Lydia shrunk away from her, her eyes huge with dread. What was Fran going to do?

'Danny . . . ?' Lydia whispered.

'Shush!' Daniel said softly.

An old-fashioned carriage clock chimed softly on a table in the room. Overhead, Lydia heard the grownups ransacking the house but the sound faded until all Lydia could hear was the tick-ticking of the carriage clock.

Is she going to kill us? Does she hate us that much? Lydia wondered, fearfully.

Without warning, Fran suddenly wielded the knife to cut the ropes binding both Lydia and Daniel.

'Don't say a word,' Fran whispered. 'We don't have much time.'

'Why're you doing this?' Daniel questioned.

'Because Lydia needs to get back to her own time and change all this,' Fran whispered.

'You believe me?' Lydia asked.

'I want to believe you. I have to believe you. If there's the slightest chance that you're telling the truth, that my mum might not die . . .' Fran answered. 'Now come on. We don't have much time.' She dug into her pocket and took out a laser gun. 'I've set it to stun. That's all you need,' she said firmly.

Daniel nodded, understanding what Fran was saying. Fran handed it over.

'Let's go,' said Daniel.

He took the lead as they tiptoed out of the room and across the hall to the front door. His face set in a worried grimace, Daniel tried to open the door. Lydia held her breath as the door began to slide open.

'Fran, what on earth . . . ? STOP!' Fran's dad stood at the top of the stairs.

'Quick!' Daniel pulled Lydia and Fran through the half-opened front door. 'My car! Over there!' he pointed.

Lydia and Fran raced for the car, parked just by the first set of trees in the wood.

'Where's Danny?' Lydia gasped as she ran. She turned her head to see him press a key on the front door's keypad, then jump to one side as a white laser bolt missed him by millimetres. Lydia froze.

'Danny! Danny, are you OK?'

'Get going!' Daniel shouted.

Lydia started running again. Daniel fired his laser gun at the door's keypad just as it slid shut, then he raced after Fran and his sister.

By now Lydia and Fran were at the car, desperately pulling at the door handles to open it but it was locked.

'Danny . . .'

'Move!' Daniel yelled as he pelted towards them.

Fran and Lydia stepped aside. Daniel pointed the transmitter on his wrist at the car. Lydia heard a click as the doors opened.

'We don't have much time,' Daniel said urgently as they all bundled into the front of the car. 'A jammed keypad won't keep them in for very long.'

'What about Old Lydia?' Lydia asked.

'She must have hidden in one of the house's secret passages. I'll come back for her but right now we have to get out of here.'

The car began to take off vertically.

'My dad's got a transmitter. He'll tell the others we've escaped,' Fran warned.

'We'll just have to take our chances,' said Daniel.

Fran turned to look out of the window. Lydia frowned at her.

'Fran, what's the matter?' she asked.

'They'll think I'm a traitor.' Tears shimmered in Fran's eyes.

Lydia took Fran's hand in her own. 'Do you think you're a traitor?' she asked.

Fran shook her head. She tried to smile, her eyes still shining with tears that began to run down her cheeks. Impatiently, Fran brushed them away with the back of her hand.

'I don't think you are either,' Lydia said.

'Thanks,' Fran whispered. After a shared smile, she asked, 'So where're we going?'

Daniel and Lydia looked at each other.

'To the moors,' Lydia replied.

Twenty-Two

Old Lydia

The car sped over the trees and headed west of Hensonville on its way to the moors.

'Fran's dad and the others didn't find Old Lydia in the house. D'you know what happened to her? Where is she?' Lydia asked.

'I don't know. I wish I did. She should be safe as long as she's not stupid enough to try and take on those thugs left in the house by herself.' Daniel sounded worried. 'The secret passages lead all over the house and grounds so she should be OK.'

'Old Lydia? Is that Lydia Henson?' Fran asked, aghast. She turned to Lydia. 'Is that . . . are you still alive? Is she the older version of you?'

Lydia looked at Daniel. 'No, she's not the older version of me. She's just someone,' she replied, still looking at her brother.

'Someone with the same name as you?' Fran said.

'Yeah, but that's all we have in common,' Lydia said firmly.

Silence.

'What will Old Lydia do now?' Lydia asked Daniel.

Daniel shrugged. 'I wish I knew. She doesn't care about much – not even you, Lydia. All she's got on her mind is making the people of this town suffer. It's strange, but it took seeing you again and remembering how things used to be to make me want something else. Something better. I couldn't care less for the people in this place. But I care very much for my family. No matter what my sister thinks, I'm doing this for her and me. No-one else.'

'Whatever the reason – you're doing it. That's what counts,' said Lydia. She smiled sadly at her brother. He still couldn't forgive the people of Tarwich for what they'd done to her. Strange that she could now and he couldn't. 'I hope I don't let you down,' she whispered.

Fran looked from one to the other but said nothing.

They flew over the Night Guards' camp. Through the window, Lydia could see laser bolts and EM rifle fire flashing through the air like red and white arrows. There was a pitched battle going on beneath them. As they flew on, Lydia could see a small breakaway division forming a separate group away from the main Resistance. They were obviously the Resistance as they weren't wearing the uniform of the Night Guards.

As the air-car flew over them, they were close enough for Lydia to see that the group was led by Anne Joyce. The breakaway division immediately pursued the car.

I'm going to change this version of the future. *I am*, Lydia told herself over and over.

'At this height they can reach up and whip off our tyres!' Fran said desperately. 'Can't you go any higher?'

'This is an air-car, not a moon shuttle,' frowned Daniel. 'If I fly much higher, the safety system will automatically cut out the engine.'

Lydia saw some of the members of the Resistance pointing their weapons up at them.

'Daniel . . .'

Without warning, the car lurched and there was a horrible crunching sound.

'Hang on!' Daniel called out.

'What's the matter?' Lydia asked, alarmed.

'We've been hit,' Fran told her.

'I'm going to have to take the chance.' Daniel pushed one of the two gear sticks in the car forward and the car rose higher into the air.

'Look!' Daniel pointed ahead.

Almost before Daniel spoke, Lydia felt the hairs on the back of her neck begin to prickle. There it was – the electric storm. But now it was only about a mile away and far bigger and more frightening than ever before. Every colour of the rainbow whirled and swirled ahead. It was as if not just the clouds but the very sky itself was burning up. Flashes of white lightning lit up the air. Every nerve in Lydia's body screamed for her to get away from it, to put as much space between her and the storm as possible. But every instinct told her to keep going.

'I don't like this . . .' Daniel studied his car's console.

'What?'

'That storm is affecting all the car's systems,' Daniel said. 'My instrument panel is going haywire.'

Lydia looked through her car door window. They were quite some distance above the ground.

'I think I'd better . . .' Daniel didn't get any further. The car began to rock violently. Daniel pulled back on one of his two gear sticks and pressed one of the foot pedals. The car flipped over to the left and almost turned over completely. Fran screamed. Lydia closed her eyes and held on to her chair until her knuckles ached.

'We're going to crash-land. Hold on,' Daniel called out.

The car spiralled round and round as it nose-dived. The ground came rushing up to meet them. Then it was as if a giant hand had reached out of the sky and pulled them back up. They were all wrenched forwards in their seats, saved only by the seatbelts. After stunned moments, Lydia looked out of the rear window. A large white parachute had opened up behind them.

Lydia and Fran hugged each other, laughing with relief.

'We're not out of the woods yet,' Daniel informed them grimly.

They only just had time to look through the front windscreen and see the ground only metres away before the car hit the ground with a colossal thump. There wasn't time to panic. There wasn't even time for Fran to let out another scream. They all lurched forward until their seatbelts snapped tight across them. If it wasn't for those, Fran and Lydia would have gone through the windscreen for sure. The front of the car was wedged a good half a metre into the ground with the rear end of the car pointing almost straight up in the air. A stunned silence descended on them as everyone held their breath, totally stunned.

'Are you two OK?' Daniel asked at last.

'Yes, I think so,' Lydia mumbled.

Fran nodded, adding, 'Let's get out of here.'

Lydia pushed at her door a number of times before it finally flew open. She swung her legs around and jumped down out of the car. Fran followed. Daniel did the same from his own side of the car.

'We'd better get going. The Resistance are close behind us,' Daniel said.

'How will you two get away from them?' Lydia asked.

'If we succeed in getting you back to your own time, we won't have to. You'll change your future and none of this as you've seen it will happen.' Daniel smiled.

The electrical storm was less than two hundred metres ahead. Looking at it dazzled Lydia's eyes and made her head ache. Muted shouting had Lydia and everyone else turning around. Approaching fast were the group from the Resistance.

'Lydia, hurry. We won't get a second chance,' Daniel said quickly.

Lydia looked from the storm to the Resistance group behind her and back again. Even racing flat out, there was no way she could reach the storm before the members of the Resistance got to Daniel and Fran. All it would take was one well-aimed blast from a laser gun and Lydia would never see 1995 again . . .

'Lydia, go!' Daniel urged.

Lydia took a deep breath. She'd have to run like she'd never run before. But before she'd even taken a step, a high-pitched whooshing sound filled the air. Lydia turned around. An air-car flew over the heads of the Resistance members and came to an abrupt landing, directly between them and Lydia, Daniel and Fran. The car door opened and slowly Old Lydia emerged.

'Lydia, get out of there. Lydia . . .' Daniel shouted out.

Old Lydia did a strange thing. She turned her head and smiled. And in that smile there was the first trace of what Old Lydia might have been, the first trace of what she once had been. The Resistance slowed and stopped several metres away from Old Lydia, unsure of who she was and what she was doing.

Old Lydia turned to Anne Joyce. Lydia heard her say something but was too far away to hear what it was. She took a step forward. Danny placed a restraining hand on her shoulder.

'Go Lydia. Go now,' Daniel told his twelve-year-old sister at his side.

'I can't leave. They'll kill her,' Lydia said.

'Not if you get back to your own time and change this. GO!'

Lydia quickly turned to Fran and hugged her.

'Thanks for your help, Fran,' Lydia said. 'You've been a true friend . . . just like your mum.'

'You're welcome,' Fran replied. 'I hope everything works out for you back in your own time.'

Lydia released her quickly, then looked up at Daniel. She had so much she wanted to say, so much she wanted to ask, but she'd run out of time. Lydia smiled. Daniel smiled back. Then he bent down and they hugged each other tightly.

'You're the best brother in the world, Danny,' Lydia whispered.

Daniel straightened up. He looked towards the storm.

'This had better work,' he said drily. 'We're all in deep trouble if it doesn't!'

Lydia laughed. She couldn't help it. She took one last look at her grown-up brother. Then as he raced forward to be with Old Lydia, the twelve-year-old Lydia turned towards the storm and *ran*. She ran like the wind, praying that she wasn't wrong about the storm, praying that she'd make it back to 1995. Behind her, Lydia heard the familiar whistle of laser-gun fire. Lydia wanted to turn around – she *burned* to see what was happening, but she forced herself not to look back. She didn't want to see Danny injured or Fran hurt or herself dead . . . Too much knowledge . . .

And still she ran.

Even though every hair on her body, every drop of blood within her, screamed for her to turn back.

Running into the storm was like stepping off into another world. A world of fire which burnt her from the inside out as she stepped into it. Just when Lydia thought she'd die from the pain, suddenly it was gone. Cool air rushed to meet her and drops of water splashed on her forehead and her cheeks.

And still Lydia ran – on and on, until it felt as if she wasn't running on the ground any more but on the very air itself. Lydia slowed and turned but the whole world was a swirling mass of colours. The air was getting colder and a high-pitched whine filled the air, getting louder. So loud in fact that Lydia had to put her hands over her ears. The wind grabbed her and tossed her up into the air as if she was on a trampoline. Lydia closed her eyes tight and held her breath. The high-pitched whine was now a painful shriek in her ears. And the rain was getting heavier. Lydia spun around and around until she had no idea which way was up.

Suddenly all sounds stopped. Lydia struggled to open her eyes but each eyelid weighed a ton. The world was perfectly dark and still. Then Lydia heard voices, faint at first but growing more distinct with each passing second. Someone was calling her.

'Lydia . . . ? Lydia . . . ?'

After a supreme effort, Lydia managed to open her eyes. Directly above her was the night sky, full of stars. Lydia tried to prop herself up using her hands, but her strength was gone. Then she realized that the ground was soaking wet. She slowly moved her fingers around. The earth was definitely wet. And she had on her winter jacket and her original shirt and jumper. Did that mean . . . ?

'Lydia . . . ? Lydia, answer us.'

'Dad . . .' The word came out in little more than a croak. Lydia coughed to clear her throat and tried again. 'DAD!'

Streams of torchlight bounced towards Lydia.

She struggled to sit up and called again, 'MUM! DAD!'

A crowd of people gathered around Lydia. Someone placed a blanket around her shoulders.

'Lydia? Lydia, darling are you all right? Speak to us. Are you hurt? Lydia?'

And all at once, there they were. Hugging her and kissing her and pushing her soaking wet hair back off her face – Lydia's mum and dad.

Twenty-Three

Back At School

The next few days were a blurry haze to Lydia. She remembered being freezing cold all the time and a flurry of people swarming around her. She remembered dropping off to sleep, only to be woken up by someone who would insist on holding her wrist to take her pulse or else on sticking a thermometer under her armpit. She remembered a constant heavy feeling on her chest that made it hurt terribly to even breathe. And all the time it was so, so cold.

Then one morning Lydia woke up and for the first time in a long time she was actually comfortable. She savoured the feeling for several seconds, feeling snug and safe. She opened her eyes and saw a bright, multi-coloured curtain hanging on one part of the rail that surrounded the bed. The ceiling and walls were cream-coloured and there was a very peculiar smell around, like flowery disinfectant.

I'm in hospital, Lydia realized.

She looked at the curtains again. The same colours and patterns swirled and spiralled on the curtains as had been present on the moors during the electrical storm.

I wasn't dreaming. I couldn't have been dreaming . . . *could I?* Lydia wondered.

But how could she tell?

My arm . . . Lydia remembered.

Pushing down the blankets that covered her, Lydia twisted her left upper arm slightly and strained her neck to see it. A large piece of lint covered her arm, kept in place by two strips of tape. Lydia peeled back one of the bits of tape, wincing as it tore some of her hairs out by the roots! And there it was – an S-shaped wound like a snake crawling across her skin.

'It *did* happen,' Lydia breathed.

'Lyddy? Lyddy, you're awake!'

Lydia heard a voice she hadn't heard in a long time. She turned her head – and there was Danny. Ten years old and just as scabby as ever.

'Danny . . .' Lydia breathed.

Danny raced from the room. 'Dad! Mum! Lyddy's awake!'

Seconds later, Lydia's family surrounded her bed.

'Lydia, how're you feeling?'

'You look a lot better . . .'

'We were frantic . . .'

They all spoke at once.

'What happened?' Lydia whispered.

'You went missing. We found you lying on the moors, soaked through to the bone and freezing cold,' said Dad.

'You've been in hospital for six days,' sniffed Mum. 'I've never been so worried.'

Dad put his arm around Mum and hugged her to him. It didn't do any good. Tears rolled down Mum's cheeks.

'You didn't have to worry, Mum,' Lydia smiled. 'Danny and I live for ages yet.'

Mum and Dad looked at each other. Lydia's eyelids fluttered shut but she forced them open again. Mum busied herself by tucking in the sheets around Lydia. Then she saw that Lydia's bandage was loose.

'You mustn't worry about that,' Mum said, pressing the tape back down onto Lydia's skin. 'You hurt your arm on the moors. You must have hit it against a rock or something. The stitches will be out soon.'

'What happened to the staples?' Lydia asked sleepily.

'What staples?' asked Dad.

Lydia smiled. 'It doesn't matter.'

She realized that the staples must have disappeared as she came back in time. That was the only explanation. As medical staples of that kind hadn't been invented yet, they couldn't really come back to 1995 with her! Lydia looked around the room. 1995 had never looked so amazing – so wonderful!

'Is . . . is Frankie awake yet?'

'Yes, as a matter of fact, she is,' said Dad. 'She woke up the day after her accident. No bones broken luckily. Just a concussion.'

'She told everyone it was an accident,' Mum added.

'If that reporter prints one word to the contrary, I'll sue him and his paper for every bloomin' penny they've got,' Dad said belligerently.

'I don't mind – not any more.' Lydia's eyelids fluttered again as she fought to stay awake.

'Danny, come here,' Lydia sighed.

Danny moved to stand in front of his mum and dad.

'Come closer,' Lydia breathed.

'Why?'

'Stop arguing with your sister. Can't you see she's sick,' grumbled Dad.

'Yeah! Sick in the head!' Danny muttered so everyone could hear him, but he did as asked and bent over Lydia so that his ear was close to her lips.

Lydia kissed his cheek, grinning broadly when he sprang back as if scalded.

'Yeuk! Yeuk!' Danny yelled, rubbing his cheek vigorously. 'Don't do that!'

'That's for being a good friend,' Lydia said.

'You're crazy!' Danny was still rubbing his cheek.

Lydia burst out laughing at the incredulous expression on her brother's face, but her laughter soon turned into a coughing fit.

'That's enough excitement for one day,' said Mum firmly. 'Lydia, get some rest. We'll see you tomorrow.'

'What's today's date?' Lydia asked, suddenly.

'The twenty-ninth of November. Why?' Dad frowned.

Lydia smiled. 'Brilliant! I can go back to school before the end of term.'

Danny looked down at his shoes. Mum and Dad exchanged a look and Lydia caught it all.

'What's the matter?' Lydia asked.

'Lydia, you're not going back to that school.' Dad's voice was rock hard. 'If they hadn't bullied you and made your life such a misery then you wouldn't have run away.'

'H-How d'you know about that?' Lydia said.

'Someone in your class finally told your teacher what was going on every breaktime,' Mum replied angrily. 'The teachers swear that they didn't know what was happening. What kind of school is that?'

'You're not going back there, and that's final,' Dad insisted.

'Who told Mr Fine what was going on?' Lydia asked.

Dad shrugged. 'I don't know. Someone with a bit more courage than the rest of them in your class.'

'Let's get off unpleasant subjects, shall we,' Mum sniffed. 'Lydia, we've got wonderful news.'

Lydia held her breath. Something told her that the news wasn't going to be as wonderful as her mum and dad thought.

'As soon as the term is over and Danny's finished school, we're all going down to your Auntie Vanessa's. We're going to spend Christmas with her in London,' smiled Mum. 'I think we've all had about enough of this town for a while.'

'How are we going to get there?' Lydia whispered.

'To your aunt's?'

Lydia nodded.

'By car of course,' Dad said.

Lydia's heart began to hammer in her chest.

'I don't want to leave Collivale School,' Lydia said slowly. 'I want to go back just as soon as I can.'

'But Lydia, you've been pestering me to go to another school ever since . . . ever since that wretched cup was found in your locker,' argued Mum.

'I know, but I've changed my mind. Please don't take me out of Collivale.'

'But . . .'

'Please . . .'

'Lydia, I don't think . . .'

'*Please.*'

'You are a strange child, Lydia.' Mum sighed.

'Does that mean I can stay at school until the end of term?' Lydia asked, tearfully.

'Yes, I suppose so. If it means that much to you,' said Mum reluctantly.

'And Dad, do we have to go to Aunt Vanessa's this Christmas?' Lydia began. 'Can't we stay in Hensonvi . . . I mean, Tarwich.'

'No, we cannot,' Dad replied. 'I've had enough of this place, even if you haven't.'

Lydia opened her mouth to argue, but then decided that now was not the time.

First things first, Lydia thought to herself.

Before anything else, she had some things to take care of back at school.

Twenty-Four

With A Little Help

Lydia took a deep breath, then another. Wiping her sweaty hand on her skirt first, she opened the classroom door. It was as if a radio had been suddenly switched off. All the chatting and laughing suddenly stopped. Lydia's face burned.

Mr Fine smiled. 'Welcome back, Lydia.'

'Thank you, sir,' Lydia replied, her voice little more than a squeak.

She looked around. All eyes were on her. Anne and Frankie were sitting together. Frankie didn't smile but she did look pleased to see Lydia, which was more than could be said for Anne.

'Sit down next to Shaun,' Mr Fine pointed.

Lydia did as she was told. Shaun pulled his chair away from Lydia and scowled at her. Lydia lowered her head. With that one little thing, Shaun still managed to get to her, even though Lydia had promised herself that she wouldn't let anyone upset her. Then Lydia remembered how Shaun had looked as a grown-up, with a balding head and a bulging beer belly, and she had to bite her lip to stop herself from laughing out loud. Lydia risked a glance around the room. Even though Mr Fine was talking, everyone was watching her. Lydia stared straight ahead. Let them stare. Lydia didn't care.

'Could Barry Finley please report to the school secretary during today's lunch break.' The school secretary's voice rang out over the PA system as she repeated the message.

Lydia shook her head. It was almost as if she'd never been away. Today was like any other school day, except for one thing.

Today, she had a number of things to set up. Before the week was over, she was going to sort this thief business once and for all. The only trouble was, she couldn't do it alone. She needed help. Would she be able to find it?

Lydia leaned against the wall outside her empty class room, her head tilted back, her eyes closed. And she waited. It'd been two days since she'd returned to school. The name calling had stopped. She was no longer surrounded in the playground and taunted. Instead, no-one but the teachers talked to her. It was as if she was a ghost that no-one could see. Conversations flowed over and around and through her. No-one stopped talking when Lydia approached any more. They didn't have to. Lydia was treated as if she just wasn't there. In a way that was even worse than before.

Lunchtime smells wafted across the quad from the canteen. They made Lydia feel slightly sick. Her heart was pounding with anticipation. This was it. The only chance she'd get to prove her innocence.

Quick footsteps echoed on the floor. Lydia opened her eyes. Anne was walking towards her. She didn't even bother to disguise the huge smirk on her face.

'I want to talk to you.' Lydia stepped out in front of her.

'I'm meant to be meeting Frankie here, not you. I don't have anything to say to you – thief!' Anne tried to step past Lydia.

Lydia blocked her way.

'Tough! 'Cause I've got plenty I want to say to you,' Lydia replied.

She grabbed Anne's arm and pushed her into the deserted classroom. Anne snatched her arm out of Lydia's grasp.

'Just what d'you think you're doing?' Anne asked indignantly.

'Anne, I know how you did it,' said Lydia.

'Did what?'

'I know how you put the cup in my locker,' Lydia said.

'Oh yeah?'

'Yeah! You unscrewed the backplate of my locker and put the sports cup in that way.'

Anne stared at Lydia, surprised. Then she pursed her lips. 'Don't talk rubbish. Look! I've had enough of this.' Anne pushed Lydia out of her way. Lydia pushed her back.

'Oh no, you don't. I want to know why you did it. D'you really hate me that much?' Lydia said. 'What did I do?'

Anne didn't reply. Lydia was getting desperate. It wasn't working.

'It's because of Frankie, isn't it? You were jealous, weren't you?'

'Me? Jealous of you? Do me a favour!' Anne snapped angrily.

'That's it . . . You were jealous,' goaded Lydia.

'Frankie is my friend, not yours,' Anne said icily. 'It served you right – trying to take Frankie away from me.'

'So you put the cup in my locker?'

'Of course I did,' Anne scoffed. 'I knew you wouldn't take it, you prissy sissy. I even slipped a message under Mr Simmers' door saying that the sports cup was in someone's locker.'

'You're a real cow, Anne!' Even though Lydia knew it was true, it was still hard for her to believe that anyone could be so spiteful.

'Call me what you like, I don't care,' laughed Anne. 'And I'm not sorry I did it either.'

'You will be,' Lydia said quietly.

'Oh yeah? Everyone reckons you're a thief and you can't prove any different,' Anne scorned.

'Yes, I can.'

'Go on then. What're you going to make me

do? Confess? You make me sick. You really are all talk and no action,' said Anne.

'I feel sorry for you, Anne.' Lydia shook her head sadly. 'We could've been really good friends.'

'I don't think so. I never liked you and now neither does anyone else. And serve you right. Now let me out of this room before I knock you down.'

Lydia stared at Anne, wondering that anyone could be so spiteful, so vicious. Anne stepped around Lydia, glowering with contempt. Lydia didn't turn back. She flinched as Anne slammed the door behind her. Less than a minute later the door opened again. In came Frankie, panting.

Lydia and Frankie watched each other silently.

'Where were you then?' Lydia asked.

'I got held up. Mrs Irving collared me in the corridor.'

'Anne's gone.'

'She confessed?'

'She didn't so much confess as boast about it,' Lydia said with disgust.

'So did it work?'

Lydia nodded. 'I think so. I hope so.'

'You stayed in the corner by the door?'

Lydia nodded. 'Yeah, just as we rehearsed.'

Silence.

'She really hates me, doesn't she,' Lydia sighed.

'Well, she's going to get what she deserves – and not a moment too soon.' Frankie's eyes narrowed with delight.

Lydia didn't reply. Now came the hardest bit – trusting Frankie to do her part . . .

'Frankie!' Mr Fine wailed.

Anne whispered something to Frankie. Frankie didn't answer. She stood up and made her way down to the front of the class. Lydia's heart was in her mouth as she watched. Frankie had doctored the VCR so that it wouldn't start properly when Mr Fine pressed the PLAY button. Hence the desperate wail! Without warning, the door opened and in walked Mr Simmers, the headmaster.

'Ah, Mr Fine, you wanted to see me?' Mr Simmers strode up to Mr Fine, his eyebrows raised in query.

Mr Fine frowned. 'I did?'

Now it was Mr Simmers' turn to frown. 'Lydia told me that you wanted to see me at the start of your English lesson,' he explained.

'She did?'

Both teachers turned to Lydia, as did everyone else in the class. Lydia stood up slowly. She glanced at Frankie who was still fiddling with the VCR.

Hurry up, Frankie! Hurry up . . .

'What's going on, Lydia?' The headmaster's frown deepened. Frost crept into his voice. 'Am I correct in thinking that you've got me here under false pretences?'

'I had to, sir,' Lydia said. 'I . . . I . . .'

The room lapsed into a deafening silence. Frankie turned around and nodded vigorously to Lydia.

Mr Simmers opened his mouth to speak.

'I've got something to show you, sir,' Lydia interrupted the headmaster quickly.

Frankie pressed the PLAY button on the VCR. The TV screen instantly flickered into life. Anne was angrily pulling her arm out of Lydia's grasp. She said something that was lost under Anne's gasp in the classroom. Frankie turned up the volume.

'I know how you put the cup in my locker,' Lydia was saying.

'Oh yeah?'

'Yeah! You unscrewed the backplate of my locker and put the sports cup in that way.'

The whole conversation, every action, every word, was displayed in glorious technicolour. Each word rang out crystal clear. Anne and Lydia were beautifully framed, slap bang in the middle of the screen. Frankie turned around to Lydia and grinned. No-one else in the class noticed. They only had eyes for the drama unfolding before them on the TV screen. And when Anne confessed to planting the cup in Lydia's locker and told why she did it, even Mr Simmers gave a sharp intake of breath.

'It's a lie. I didn't say that. I didn't . . .' Anne sprang to her feet.

The conversation between Anne and Lydia finished. Black and white static lines filled the screen. They cleared suddenly to reveal the middle of an episode of *Coronation Street*! Frankie pressed the STOP button.

'Mr Simmers, I can play it again if you like. Lydia and I set up my dad's camcorder this lunchtime and taped Anne bragging about what she did. Then I ran home and transferred it on to a VHS tape.'

'I didn't do it . . .' Anne denied weakly.

'I didn't take the cup, Mr Simmers. Anne did. I just never had any proof until now,' Lydia explained quietly.

'Give me that tape,' Mr Simmers said grimly.

Frankie pressed the EJECT button and handed the tape over to the headmaster.

'Anne, come with me. And you as well, Lydia. And you, Frankie,' Mr Simmers continued. 'You've all got a lot of explaining to do.'

'I told you Lyddy didn't do it,' said Danny proudly. 'I hope that other girl gets suspended!'

'They won't do that. Frankie told me that Anne's mum is one of the school's governors!' said Lydia.

'Tell me what happened again!' Danny said eagerly.

'But I've already told you four times,' Lydia protested.

'Tell me again,' Danny pleaded.

'Mr Simmers played the tape in his office and Anne tried to deny it. She said that Frankie and me had doctored the tape. Then she said that she was just playing up to me and, when that didn't work, she even tried to say that it was Frankie pretending to be her on the tape!'

Danny sat back and laughed like a drain at that, even though he'd heard it before.

'And then when that didn't work, she started crying to get Mr Simmers' sympathy. She didn't have much luck with that either!' Lydia said with satisfaction. 'Mr Simmers sent me and Frankie back to our class and, as we were leaving, he was phoning Anne's parents.'

'She should get expelled, not suspended,' Danny said vehemently.

'You said it!' Mum and Dad spoke in unison and nodded in vigorous agreement, their heads moving at exactly the same time.

They turned to each other and burst out laughing. The Henson household was back to normal. Ever since Mum and Dad had received the news that the real thief had been found, it was as if all the windows in the house had been thrown wide open, letting in daylight and fresh air after weeks of darkness. Mum and Dad were actually laughing again.

'It's funny but . . . I feel a bit sorry for Anne,' Lydia sighed.

Danny's jaw dropped open. 'You must be joking !' he exclaimed.

'I know what it's like to have everyone hating you and not talking to you. I wouldn't want her to go through the same thing,' said Lydia.

Danny shook his head, amazed. Mum and Dad looked at each other.

'Besides, I wouldn't want Hensonville to become . . . Turnerville !' Lydia smiled.

'Lydia, what on earth are you talking about?' Mum frowned.

'It doesn't matter, Mum. I'm just wittering to myself. Maybe I'll try and be friends with Anne again,' Lydia mused. 'And then again, maybe I won't ! I'll have to see.'

'I'm just glad the whole thing is sorted out now,' sighed Dad.

'Dad . . .'

The phone rang, interrupting Lydia.

'I'll be right back,' said Mum.

'What were you going to say, Lydia?' Dad asked.

Lydia chewed on her bottom lip. She should be happy but she wasn't. The sports cup theft at school was all cleared up but that still left the accident on the motorway . . . Lydia's heart leapt at the thought of it. Should she risk telling Mum and Dad what she knew about the future? It sounded so bizarre, so far-fetched that they'd never believe her. Even now Lydia wondered if she'd been knocked out and just dreamt the whole thing or had it really happened? Yes, there was the scar on her arm, but what if that really had happened when she was knocked unconscious? So maybe she was worrying about nothing. But even so . . .

'Who was that?' Dad asked when Mum came back into the room.

'That was Mr Weldon, Frankie's dad,' said Mum. 'He's invited all of us to spend Boxing Day with his family.'

'That's nice of him,' Dad said drily.

'Are we going to go?' asked Mum.

'Oh please! Please, can we?' Lydia pleaded.

'What about your Aunt Vanessa?' Dad frowned.

'Couldn't we see her some other time?' Lydia asked.

She held her breath as she waited for Dad's answer.

'I suppose we could always visit my sister for the New Year,' said Mum. 'It would be nice to get to know some of the people in this town a bit better – if we're going to stay here, that is.'

Mum and Dad looked at each other.

'Oh, I think we'll settle down here,' said Dad at last.

Mum grinned. 'Good!'

'That's not good – that's great!' Lydia sprung out of her chair and whirled around. 'We're not going to Aunt Vanessa's before my birthday.

We're not going! We're not going!'

'And just what's wrong with my sister?' Mum frowned.

'Nothing!' Lydia grinned. 'I . . . I just didn't want to see her before my birthday, that's all.'

'Why?'

'Because I love Tarwich. I'm going to live here for ever and ever. Come here, Danny, and I'll give you a big kiss!' Lydia beamed.

'You must be drunk!' Danny retorted.

'Danny, that's a charming thing to say to your sister.' Mum raised an eyebrow.

'Well, Lydia's gone all dripping wet ever since she got out of the hospital,' Danny grumbled. 'I wish she'd stop being nice to me. I'm not used to it!'

'Danny, as I've already told you – you're the best brother in the world.'

'You've never told me that,' Danny denied.

'Oh yes, I did. I told you when you were forty-seven years old,' smiled Lydia.

'Huh?'

'And what's more, I meant it!' said Lydia.

And she did!

THE END